MISTLETOE AND MISCHIEF

MELISSA IVERS

Copyright © 2021 by Melissa Ivers

All rights reserved.

No part of this book may be reproduced or used in any form or by any electronic or mechanical means, including information storage and retrieval systems, without written permission from the author, except for the use of brief quotations in a book review. For more information, email address: melissa.ivers.author@gmail.com

This is a work of fiction. The names, characters, businesses, places, events, locales, and incidents are the products of the author's imagination or have been used fictitiously and are not to be construed as real. Any resemblance to actual persons, living or dead, actual events, locales or organizations is entirely coincidental.

Mistletoe and Mischief

Cover Designer: CT Cover Creations

Formatting: KM Rives

For the readers who need a Christmas miracle

1
JULIA

❄

Drunken frat boys dancing through the bar, waving their hands like they just don't care, and singing their interpretation of *Jingle Bell Rock* does not get me into the Christmas spirit. It does very little to instill holiday joy and cheer. It does, however, have my teeth grinding together as they get on each and every one of my nerves.

I sigh, rather dramatically, tucking my legs under the lip of the bar, and taking long relaxing sips from my Manhattan.

Well, long sips anyway. Not sure I'm to the point of relaxing yet.

Don't get me wrong, Christmas is a wonderful time of year. Tis the season to be jolly and all that. But the holiday season doesn't hold the same joy for me as it does others. Not anymore. Christmas hasn't been the same since my parents died five years ago.

Instead of wasting my time decorating and crafting, I throw myself into work, and lucky for me, Christmas is my busy season. I've been up to my asshole in cake and cookies for weeks. I'm not the only baker in Aspen, but my shop, Sweet Pies, is the best. And yes, that's the general opinion, not just mine. My ratings on all the local food blogs are always consistent and between a four point five and five stars. Everyone knows, the internet is never wrong.

Except for that one guy who thought my lemon tart was too tart. It's right there in the name, sweetheart. It's not my fault you can't read. It's supposed to be tart. He obviously didn't know his head from his ass.

"Do you want another?"

I lift my gaze to Rebecca, the only bartender at Breck's who knows how to make a decent Manhattan, and swirl the ice in my empty glass. That can't be good. I didn't even realize I'd drained it. I should pay better attention; I don't need to end up hammered.

There's too much to do tomorrow, and trying to decorate cakes with a hangover is never a good idea. I'm still horrified by the expression on Mrs. Castle's face when she came to pick up an elephant cake for her son and refused to leave with it because it looked like a giant dick.

It was, however, a hit at the bachelorette party happening the same weekend.

"Sure. Just one more." I'm not even feeling a buzz from the first one, so a second won't hurt.

"You got it. Anything for the woman who aids my cookie addiction."

She tosses me a wink over her shoulder, and I can't help but laugh. You wouldn't be able to tell from her petite frame and small waist, but the girl stops by the bakery every Friday for a dozen cookies.

I prop my elbow on the bar and rest my chin in my cupped palm, wishing I didn't have to open the shop at the ass crack of dawn. While I like to keep busy, the week before Christmas is brutal. Two more days until Christmas Eve and I'm guaranteed to work my fingers to the proverbial bone.

"Here you go, Jules."

"Thanks." I accept the new Manhattan and take a small sip, careful not to drink it too fast. "Rowdy crowd tonight. I don't know how you do it. This amount of noise all day, every day, would drive me crazy."

Rebecca winks before flashing me a grin. "It's nothing I can't handle. Just need to supply the tourists with a steady flow of craft beer and flirtatious smiles. Perky boobs don't hurt either."

I laugh, putting my back to the bar, and looking over the crowd. They're out in droves. Not just because it's a Friday night, but because it's the last one before Christmas—meaning the tourists are fucking loud and grating on my nerves, acting like their mothers raised them with no manners.

The Christmas carols blaring over the jukebox only amplifies the obnoxiousness. It gives the drunks ample opportunity to show off their musical talent with their own renditions of *Winter Wonderland* and *Frosty the Snowman*. As expected, the musical stylings of man-boys aren't even close to the originals. You can find all types of people and apparently, talent, at Breck's.

A group of college-aged men, occupying a table by the bar, swivel their heads in my direction. All five sets of sleazy eyes settle on me, roaming over my body, and giving me the creeps. *No, thank you.*

That's my cue to turn around and mind my own damn business. I'm way too busy and have no desire to knock boots with some punk college kid skiing the slopes on Daddy's dime. At twenty-seven, I'm too old for all the frat boy, drunken bullshit.

A heavy hand lands on my shoulder and I tense.

"What the—"

"Hey, Jules." My brother, Sebastian, wraps his long arms around me and pulls me to his chest for a tight hug. "I stopped by the house to drop off my suitcase and you weren't there."

The insult loaded on my tongue dies as I bury my face in his shoulder to return his hug, squeezing him like I haven't seen him in almost a year. Which I haven't. We've been too busy to get together even though we live close. My brother, business lawyer extraordinaire, moved to Denver right out of law school to open his own practice. A practice that does quite well, and if it weren't for his partner, it'd be perfect.

"What? No hug for me, Sweets?"

As if a single thought could spawn the Devil himself.

Steel replaces the bone in my spinal column, my blood simmers, and my pulse hammers against my veins. That deep melodic voice belongs to Sebastian's snarky law partner, best friend, and the man who's like a brother to him—but the bane of my existence. *Nashton Wyatt.* Much to my chagrin, he's an Aspen native with most of his family still living here. When my brother comes home for a visit, he has a tendency to follow. Much like a brainless lemming.

Nashton is cocky. Bossy. Arrogant. Perfect for the spawn of Satan that he is.

Qualities that I'm sure make him a renowned lady killer, though I'm not sure why. I guess his light brown hair, styled short, is the perfect length for wandering fingers to muss. Not mine, of course. He can muss his own damn hair. He's good-looking for an asshole, with his disgustingly gorgeous sky-blue eyes and pretentious cheekbones. If you like that sort of thing. Which I certainly do not. I much prefer my men with a little bit of integrity and, at the very least, a soul.

Sebastian whispers against my ear. "Be nice, Jules. You know I don't like it when you guys fight."

I scoff. There's no way I'm going to be anything even resembling nice. My ability to be pleasant to Nash disappeared as soon as we met.

He came over to the house a few weeks after they started middle school. Nash was new in town and he and my brother became instant friends. I thought he had a cute smile...until he tripped me in the backyard, laughed as I fell and then pulled my pigtails. We've been fighting ever since. Although my brother has gotten better, he was no innocent bystander, and the two of them liked pranks. Nothing was ever safe. They rigged Mentos inside my pop bottles, changed out hand sanitizer for lube, and even gave me a caramel-coated onion. I still have nightmares about that one. Let me tell you, once you bite into one of those, you'll never eat a caramel apple ever again.

"Tell that to him," I mumble under my breath.

"I heard that." Nash sticks his hand in my hair and tousles it like I'm five-years-old. If he's not careful, he's gonna lose that hand. I'll bite it off myself. "I'm always nice."

"Unless you're beating the shit out of my boyfriends. Or breathing."

"You're impossible." Nash crosses his arms in a huff.

He is impossible.

"Fuck off." I step out of my brother's arms, give Nash a light shove, and let out a frustrated sigh because he doesn't budge an inch. *Why does he have to have so many muscles?* And trust me, I know he does. The man runs around shirtless half the time and the other half wears t-shirts that like to ride up every single damn time he raises his arms. I don't have to look, I know that, but that's like telling an artist not to admire the Mona Lisa. Doesn't mean I have to like him. "Did you guys stop by to pick me up?"

"Of course." Sebastian grabs my glass and drains the remaining liquid in one long gulp. He better be paying for that. "We just got to town, thought we could hang out at the house before turning in for the night. Are you still working tomorrow?"

I nod. "Yeah, but I'm closed Christmas Eve until the twenty-sixth."

Sebastian signals for Rebecca, and after paying my tab, leads the way out of the bar. Sebastian and Nash disappear out the front door and between my short legs and the Manhattan, I struggle to catch up. As I skirt around the frat boy table, one of them gets up and heads my way. *Keep walking junior. This won't end well for you.* Doesn't matter if he has the dick and moves of a porn star—I'm not interested.

"Hey, darlin'." A meaty guy with a man bun and a Texas accent grabs my hand and pulls me into him, chest to chest. His arms snake around my waist and he holds me close. "Where do you think you're runnin' off to? We haven't had the chance to get acquainted. I was just about to come over and say hi."

I bring my hands up to his chest and push. Hard. He doesn't even flinch. What is he, a fucking boulder? His grip tightens, drawing me closer, his hands resting on my very lower back. Another inch and he'd be in ass country. My eyes narrow and I level him with the heated glare I generally reserve for Nash. "I don't think what I do or where I go is any of your concern."

"Oh, I'm mighty concerned."

I shiver as his lecherous eyes fall to my cleavage before moving back up to meet my own. I guess this Texas asshole doesn't understand what it means when a woman isn't interested.

"I can show you a better time than either of those guys you're leaving with."

Struggling against him, I fail to get out of his hold. "Let me go."

"I don't think so." He smiles wide, his hot breath

hitting me in the face, reeking of stale beer and cigarette smoke. If he's looking to get his dick wet, he'd be better off finding a toothbrush first.

"I suggest you let her go. Right. Fucking. Now." Nash's voice booms over my shoulder. It's terse and full of authority. A voice that promises retribution if it's crossed. It's deep and gruff and...downright sexy?

Wait, what?

Sexy? That can't be right.

Disgusting, putrid, and nauseating. But never sexy.

Texas boy quirks his lips to a smile, peering over my head, challenge glinting in his beady little eyes. "Is that so? And who the fuck are you?"

Not someone you want to mess with, I can assure him of that. Back in the day, he and my brother had been known as Smash and Bash. Not only because kids loved clever nicknames, but because they had a penchant for fighting. They may have traded their theoretical boxing gloves for hand cream and a lawyer suit, but that doesn't mean Nash has forgotten how to fight. He'd been good. Damned good. I'd seen too many kids with busted faces courtesy of the two of them to believe something like that just went away.

"Her boyfriend." Nash snakes his arms around my waist and tugs me away from Texas Boy, my back pressing against his broad muscular chest. One hand grips my hip while his other splays across my stomach possessively, his thumb grazing the underside of my breast. He nuzzles his stubbled chin against the side of my head before laying a light kiss on my temple. His lips are soft against my skin, and I stifle a moan as I lean my head to the side—playing along, of course, not because I liked it.

Jeez, that Manhattan must be hitting me harder than I realized.

What in the world is happening? Did the floor of the bar open up and drop me into *The Twilight Zone?* Yeah, Nash is a little bossy—but possessive? Over me?

Where the fuck is Sebastian?

I slant into him, ignoring the nervous fluttering in my stomach, and the swearing in my head. Texas Boy appears skeptical. Hell, I'm skeptical. After several seconds of tense silence, while the two of them do nothing but stare at each other, he nods and sulks back to his table.

I spin around to face Nash, point a finger to his chest, and speak low enough so no one would overhear. "What the hell do you think you're doing?"

The muscle in his jaw ticks, his deep blue eyes narrow on me, and I fight to ignore the weight of his hands resting on the small of my back. "Saving your ass."

"Where's Sebastian?"

"Getting the car. I came back to check on you when you didn't follow us out. Come on, *your boyfriend* is hungry and ready to get out of this dump." He spanks my ass, leaving a delicious burn on my skin.

I jump against him, completely taken off guard as our nether regions rub together for three seconds too long. I could've sworn I felt something hard against my thigh, but it must've been either my imagination or a penis shaped cell phone. "You can't just—"

"Slap your ass?" He smirks, trailing his hands over my hips, and giving them a squeeze before letting them drop to his sides. "I can and I did. You can pretend all you want that you didn't like it."

"I didn't like it." I cross my arms in a huff, stomping out the door with Nash close behind. Cocky bastard. Thinks he can slap my ass anytime he wants. Better yet, thinks he can slap my ass and I'll like it. I'll show him.

"What took you two so long?" Sebastian asks as I climb in the backseat of his Lexus.

"Some d-bag—"

"Thought I was someone else and started asking me questions," Nash interrupts, glaring at me over his shoulder. "It took him a minute to realize I was not his long-lost Army pal."

I narrow my eyes, cross my arms over my chest, and, after a few seconds of scrutiny, give him a tight nod. My brother can be a bit overprotective of me, so it's probably for the best he doesn't know what happened. He'd run in there in two seconds flat and knock that guy on his ass. Half his friends, too. No one wants to see a Smash and Bash reunion tonight. Besides, I don't have cash on me for bail money. And I've needed it before with the two of them.

"So, are we dropping Nash off on the way?" I click my seatbelt together and glance toward Nash in the passenger seat.

Sebastian slaps the steering wheel. "Shit. I'm sorry. I forgot to mention, Nash is crashing with us. His parents have some extended family staying at their place, and it's crowded over there."

Nash turns around and pins me with a sly smirk and a wink. My heart drops into my stomach, and I try to swallow past the lump in my throat.

Great.

I'd love to spend the entire Christmas holiday with my nemesis. My ocean-eyed, broad-shouldered, full-lipped nemesis.

"Perfect."

2

NASH

❄

I DON'T KNOW what it is about Julia Rowe, but I love—no, I live to get under her skin. Her cheeks redden while her chest flushes, and those whiskey eyes flash in anger, piercing through me, making me feel alive. I have a hunch she secretly enjoys fighting with me too. She goads me into it each and every time.

The look on her face when her brother dropped the bomb was priceless. I didn't expect her to take it well. In fact, I'd have been disappointed if she were happy. There's no way in hell she wants to be under the same roof with me for even one night. I stifle a laugh. It's going to be a fun holiday vacation.

For me.

I creep into the kitchen, sneaking up behind Jules, and before she can run off, I place my hands down on the countertop on either side of her, caging her in.

"What are you doing in here, Sweets? Hiding from me?"

Jules spins around and pushes at my chest, but I don't budge. It's cute she thinks she can move me. "What are you doing? Of course, I'm hiding from you. Back the fuck up. You're in my personal space."

"Not a chance." I lean forward, putting my mouth by her ear, and burying my nose in her golden blonde hair. It smells like peaches, and I fight the urge to find out if she smells like peaches everywhere. Just thinking about burying my face in that sweet pussy has my dick thickening in my jeans. "Just wanted to check on my girlfriend. Make sure you're doing okay after being groped in the bar."

Jules pushes at me again and, this time, I take a step back. I don't need her brushing into my erection and getting the wrong idea. I doubt the excuse 'it's not what you think' will work very well. There's only one reason for a hard dick, and I don't need her to know being close to her turns me on. It would only give her ammo to use against me, and that's one game I won't play. It would end with her underneath me and I can't be having that.

"You and I both know I'll never be your girlfriend. And the only person who groped me was you," she hisses as her nostrils flare and her hands fist at her sides.

I chuckle, provoking her further. She's adorable all pent up like this. Someone needs to give her a release—and fuck—I want that someone to be me. I want it to only ever be me. Too bad Sebastian made me promise years ago never to touch her. Even though I can't have her, and it drives me crazy, I can't help but get close to her every chance I get. "Don't pretend you didn't like my hands on you."

"Listen, you arrogant douche canoe." She steps forward so we're only separated by a few inches, and presses her index finger to my chest, directly over my cold heart. "The next time you put your hands on me, I'll chop them off."

I glance at her finger, which she yanks back and lets fall to her side. "Relax, Sweets. I'm fucking with you. I don't need to grope Sebastian's little sister at a dive bar in Aspen. I get enough pussy. I'm not hard up for anything. Especially you."

Her mouth slams shut so fast her teeth clack together. Her eyes harden, her lips roll inward and flatten like she's trying to hold in her insults.

Perfect. It's easier to resist her if she hates me. Otherwise, I'd give into temptation and do something stupid. Like kiss her perfect pouty lips or run my hands over the cheeks of her ass and let her feel *everything* I have to offer. "I just wanted to see if you had something to eat. I'm hungry, remember?"

Her eyes flash, and she reaches on the counter, feeling around behind her. "I'm not your personal chef. Get one of your whores to make you something."

My triumphant smile only lasts three seconds before her hand shoots up and a white cloud pelts me in the face. She shoves past me, blowing out a long breath, her anger barely contained in that petite body of hers. I stand still, staring at the open bag of flour, completely dumbfounded.

I've been antiqued. Something I've seen online, but never experienced. I don't recommend it.

There's one silver lining to getting a fistful of flour to the face. Next to the offending bag is a full plate of gingersnap cookies. My favorite.

"I bet one of my whores would love to make me a sandwich," I mutter to myself before thrusting a cookie into my eager mouth.

That'll never happen, though. I never see them twice. I don't have time for a relationship, so I don't indulge in them. Period. The women I hook up with know the deal upfront. It's about sex and mutual orgasms for one night only. I won't call the next day, and if I see one of them on the street, I keep walking. Does it make me a bastard? Probably. Too bad I don't care.

Snagging several more cookies, I stroll into the living room and drop on the edge of the worn coffee-colored leather armchair. Sebastian, who's sprawled along the length of the matching couch, looks at me, his mouth open in surprise. No doubt because I look like a Halloween ghost costume fail. I just need a little black face paint under the eyes to perfect my undead appearance.

"First of all, where did you get those cookies?"

"Kitchen. They're good. You should get off your ass and get some."

Sebastian sticks out his hand and wiggles his fingers.

Chapter 2

With an eye roll, I relinquish two. Only because he's my best friend. I don't give my cookies out to just anyone who tries to tempt me with dancing fingers.

He shoves a whole one in his mouth and speaks while chewing. "I'm not even going to ask why you're covered in flour. I know you were in there fucking with my sister. Again."

"Fuck with your sister?" I place my hand over my heart and gasp in mock horror. "I would never do that."

He shakes his head and chuckles. "You're a dick. What did I say about my sister? Off limits, dude."

My jaw clenches at his reminder. The one he'll never let me forget. "I know." All too well, in fact. Julia will never be mine. Doesn't matter that I've pined after her for years. Doesn't matter that the nameless girls that frequent my bed can't hold a candle to her. Doesn't matter if I'll never truly be happy.

When Sebastian figured out what I did all those years ago and how I felt about her, it was over for me. Fucking Colby Jenkins. The bastard deserved everything he got. Jules thought she loved that asshole—maybe she did—but I refused to sit back and watch her heart break slowly while he had his tongue down another girl's throat.

That was the day I sealed my fate. I lost my shit, fucked him up, and forced him to end his charade of a relationship with Jules on the spot. Sebastian made me promise not to tell her the truth because it would destroy her.

So, I let her think I was some asshole who wanted

nothing more than to ruin her happiness. It was better for her to think I was the bad guy, the one who hurt her, instead of that fucker breaking her. At least then, she'd only be hurt. And she could move on quickly from that.

Sebastian watched me closely after the incident, and then we had the talk. You know the one. Where he reminded me I was a player, that I didn't want a relationship, and his sister wasn't some bimbo I could use and discard. He warned me if I ever used her like that, if I ever broke her heart, I was a dead man walking. If I ever touched her, he'd kill me himself. I believed him, too. Still do.

But we aren't kids anymore, and I'm getting tired of being the bad guy.

No longer hungry, I hand Sebastian the rest of my cookies and push up from the chair. "Gonna take a shower."

"Good. Not only do you smell, but you look like a dumbass."

"Helpful. Super helpful."

I stomp up the stairs to the bathroom but can't find any damn towels. Running a hand through my hair, I sigh. I need to ask Jules for one unless I want to stand in her guest bathroom all night with my balls hanging out to air dry. It's been a long fucking day and I need a bed.

Her bedroom door is closed, no surprise, and I rap my knuckles against the wood.

"What do you need, Sebastian?" Her voice sounds

nice through the door. Never get to hear that version anymore. "This better be you and not Nash."

"It's definitely not Nash."

The knob turns and she opens the door hesitantly, taking me in with a shit-eating grin on her face. "You look good, Not Nash. White really is your color. Brings out that icy blue of your eyes and goes perfect with that dead heart of yours."

"Hilarious." I frown, looking down at my flour coated shirt. "I couldn't find any towels and suddenly find myself in dire need of a shower."

She brushes past me, her shoulders grazing my arm, and smirks. "I'll get you one. I'd say I'm sorry, but I'm not."

Neither am I. Not really. A messy shirt is a small price to pay for a moment alone with Jules. Even to trade insults.

"So, I noticed you don't have any Christmas decorations up. Been busy?" I shove my hands in my pockets and rock on my heels as I watch her open up the closet at the end of the hall. I'm not a total dick. Mostly. I care for her and want her to be happy, even if it's without me.

Jules used to love Christmas and if it weren't for the snow on the ground and lights on other people's houses, you'd have no idea the holiday is right around the corner.

She turns toward me with a stack of maroon towels, a furrowed brow, and a suspicious glint in her stare. Maybe because I'm rarely not poking the bear. Her gaze moves from the floor to my shirt, but she refuses to meet my eyes. She's silent for several seconds before she lets out a long sigh. "Yes and no. I mean, I have everything in the basement, but I haven't decorated since my parents died. I don't know. It feels stupid to say it out loud, but it doesn't feel like Christmas without them. The only reason Sebastian comes back every year is so I'm not alone, and he's never been much for decorating. It doesn't seem worth the effort."

I nod because...well, what the fuck can I say to that? I want to wrap her up in a hug and tell her how sorry I am that her parents are gone, and she'll never be alone. But there's no way I can say any of that. She hates me —I have no doubt—and I refuse to let something stupid, like my feelings, ruin my friendship with the best friend I ever had. All for another notch on my bedpost.

Although Jules would never be just some notch. She's too good for something like that. She's too good for me.

Not that it matters, so I do the only thing I can. I grab the towels with a brief thank you and pretend not to see the tears glistening in her amber eyes and highlighting the gold flecks around her irises before I retreat to the bathroom.

My feelings for her run deep and are therefore problematic. Jules can only be mine for a night, I don't do more than that, and she's not a one-night kind of girl. I know this, but it doesn't stop me from wanting her anyway. Doesn't matter though. I made a promise to her brother I can never break.

I place the towels on the countertop with a sigh and

scrub my face with my hands, wiping the flour from my eyes.

Jules has the potential to make my life complicated, and I don't do complicated very well. She's the only woman who's ever made me want to be more. To be a better man. To be good enough.

But I can never be that guy. I can never be more.

3

NASH

❄

After rolling out of bed and throwing on a pair of jeans and a white long-sleeved Henley, I go downstairs in search of Sebastian. I need to fix the Christmas thing with Jules. I may be little more than a selfish playboy, but I can try to make her Christmas special again. I wanted to have this conversation with Sebastian last night, but by the time I finished with my shower, he'd already gone to bed.

"I think we have a problem with your sister." I drop myself down on the couch next to him and run a hand through my hair.

His eyes, the same amber color as his sister's, harden as he studies my face. "Do you care to rephrase? You don't have anything with my sister."

Of course, he'd jump to conclusions after feeling the need to remind me yesterday to stay away from Jules. I lean back, letting myself sink into the plush cushions. "Pull the stick out of your ass, Bash. I'm serious."

His expression softens when he realizes I'm not trying anything he'd deem inappropriate. "I'm listening."

"Have you noticed Jules doesn't really celebrate Christmas anymore?" I sigh, sitting forward, resting my elbows on my thighs.

"I mean, I noticed she doesn't put up the trees. I didn't think much of it. Figured she was too busy with the bakery. Hell, you've seen my apartment. You know I'm not into decorating."

Sebastian looks around the room, no doubt taking in the lack of holiday décor. Bash isn't always the most observant guy. He tends to be more big picture while I handle the details.

I clear my throat, drawing his attention back to me. "She hasn't celebrated since your parents died. Doesn't feel the holiday spirit. She thinks the only reason you come back here is so she's not alone."

"Well, that's not entirely true. I don't want her to be here alone, yes, but I wouldn't want to be anywhere else. She's family. She's all I have left."

"We know that, but she doesn't. Do you remember how into Christmas she used to be? When we were in high school, she used to make us wear Santa hats while we helped her leave out cookies for Santa. And remember those ridiculous pictures she used to make us take to make cards out of?"

As teenagers, we'd been reindeers, wise men, snowmen, elves, and my least favorite, angels. It wouldn't have been so bad if she hadn't made us wear dresses. My argument that there were obviously boy angels fell on deaf ears. So, Bash and I posed for the picture, and I set out to destroy every copy she made. I think I got them all. It was a busy Christmas.

Sebastian laughs, holding a hand to his chest as he leans forward. "Those were the worst. Not as bad as the time she made us be in the live manger. Although, I did make a pretty badass Joseph."

That was the year of the wise man. Jules' favorite idea—making a recreation of the nativity scene. Bash thought he was so cool as Joseph. He paraded around in the costume all day, ordering us around as the father of Jesus. He would've kept it up all weekend, except his mom slapped him upside his head and told him he was going to Hell if he didn't stop.

"You were, hands down, the worst Joseph that ever existed." I lean back and bring a hand to my mouth to stifle a laugh. "Christ, she used to have four trees in the house. Which, by the way, is still three too many." A weight fills my chest realizing how much she's lost. "Now she doesn't even have a wreath on the door."

Sebastian furrows his brows and scrunches up his nose, it's his concentration face. Looks more like a constipation face, if you ask me, but no one ever does. "I never thought I'd say this, but you're right. She used to go nuts for Christmas. I'm so stupid. I can't believe I didn't make a connection."

"You lost your parents, too. Both of you have been dealing with things your own way, but maybe you've been existing with each other and not necessarily helping each other."

"Jesus." He runs a hand through his hair, causing half of it to stand on end. "When did you become a fucking therapist?"

I shrug. "I've known you for a long time. Both of you. I know you both went through some shit when you lost your parents, but I didn't realize it was this bad."

"I'm sorry I jumped up your ass. Christmas hasn't been the easiest since the accident and, as you pointed out, I've had my head up my ass. We should bring up some of the stuff from the basement. At the very least, we need a tree."

"Agreed." I'm not sure if a tree is good enough, but it's a good start. "We could surprise her with dinner?"

Sebastian raises his eyebrows and cocks his head to the side.

"Okay, fine." I raise my hands in concession. That might not be the best idea. Neither one of us are known for our culinary expertise. He once scorched a pan trying to boil water, and I'm not much better. "We'll order take out. I don't have much to do today. I'm waiting on instructions from—speak of the devil—my mother."

I dig my ringing phone out of my back pocket. The ringtone is one I picked to drive my mom crazy, the theme song to Golden Girls. She thinks I'm an ass. I think I'm clever.

Sebastian pushes up from the couch with a grunt. "I'm going to start going through the shit in the basement."

I nod before answering. "Hello, Mother. What a nice surprise."

"I'm sure it is, since I told you yesterday, I'd be calling. I need you to stop by Sweet Pies today and pick up the cheesecakes I ordered for the party." Straight to the point. That's my mom. She's never been a woman to waste time with pleasantries, especially when her annual ugly sweater Christmas party is on the line. She claims it's fun to get everyone together for a party, but really, she likes to torture me with light-up reindeer sweaters.

"I can do that."

"Can you see if she has time to make something else? I'm thinking I'd like some brownies or cookies to go along with the cheesecakes. The caterers are handling everything but dessert."

"I'll ask."

"Excellent. Now, what do you think about the outside lights? I was thinking I might need to add more."

Her decorations rival the most decorated houses in any Christmas movie ever made. Anymore and I'm afraid she'll either short circuit the entire neighborhood or set her house on fire.

"For the love of God, I don't think you need more lights." I move my phone from one hand to the other, switching ears. "There's no reason we need to be able to see your house from space. I know it's hard to believe, but there's such a thing as too much."

"You're no fun." She clucks her tongue. "I guess the lights I have are fine. And don't worry about finding a sweater, I've got one for you and Sebastian. You're both going to love them."

I smile into the phone. At least I won't be the only one looking like an idiot in front of the whole town. She picked out our sweaters last year too, and I wasn't sure she could top humping reindeer. "Perfect. I'm sure they're hideous."

Her musical laugh sounds through the phone. "The absolute worst. See you tomorrow, Nashton. Love you."

"Love you too, Mom." I hang up the phone and slide it in my back pocket.

I shout my goodbyes down the basement and as I'm shoving my arms in the sleeves of my jacket, a smile slowly spreads across my face. Going to Sweet Pies to pick up goodies for my mom gives me an excuse to drop in for my favorite pastime.

Needling my little sweet pie.

4

JULIA

❄

I'D BEEN PREPARED to run around like the proverbial chicken with its head cut off. What I didn't expect is to be so buried that I'm jealous of a decapitated chicken. Wouldn't be so bad if Marcy had shown up to work like she was supposed to. Although if I'm honest, the fact she finally flaked isn't the least bit surprising. I've been waiting for it, but figured she'd have the decency to wait until after the New Year.

I'm supposed to close at four thirty, but with four and a half hours left and the custom cake orders that still need to be finished, there's no way I'll be leaving until tonight. I sigh, and box another dozen red velvet cupcakes.

The door chimes and I don't spare it a glance as I pass the long white box, complete with my logo, to the soccer mom who'd been patiently waiting. "Hope you enjoy and have a merry Christmas."

"That's a good look for you, Jules."

Nash. In my head—because I'm a professional—I groan and roll my eyes. Freaking shoot me now. Just what I need. Nash to bother the fuck out of me when I'm elbows deep in work. Of course, he looks all put together in his dark jeans and charcoal button up wool jacket, and I'm sure I'm the walking definition of a hot mess. I can feel my hair coming out of my bun, and I'm positive there's frosting smudged on me somewhere. Ask me if I give a single fuck.

The three ladies in front of Nash are still browsing the case so I smooth a hand down the front of my Sweet Pies apron and walk down to the end of the display. I stop in front of him, cross my arms over my chest, and give him a look daring him to piss me off. "What are you doing here? If you've come to harass me, it'll have to wait."

He gazes around the shop before he eyes narrow on me. "Are you here by yourself? Where's your help?"

I tuck an errant hair behind my ear. "She didn't show up this morning. As you can see, I'm extremely busy."

I turn and walk back to the register where two of the ladies look ready to order. After boxing up some cookies and truffles, I eye Nash. His brows are pinched together, in his thinking face, as he regards the shop.

His gaze meets mine and he runs a hand through his hair. "How long are you open?"

"Four thirty. But there's so much to get done I'll probably be here until late." It's going to be a long day and I'm already exhausted. Not that I would tell him any of that.

"And if you had help?"

My eyes shift to the clock then back to his. "If I had help, I might be able to get enough done to leave on time. But I'm not counting on Marcy coming in. I'll probably never see her again."

I glance at the customer, browsing the display, while the door chimes as two more people come in. Nash skirts around the undecided woman and steps behind the counter.

I run over to him and hiss, "what do you think you're doing?"

Nash pulls off his winter coat revealing a long sleeve white Henley underneath. It stretches across his chest, highlighting his muscles. My eyes widen slightly, and I try to swallow with my now constricted throat. You don't get those bad boys sitting behind the desk every day. I'm momentarily lost in thought, thinking about smoothing my hands over his bare chest and around his shoulders, before I shake myself back to reality.

He hangs the pink apron around his neck and ties it at his narrowed waist. "What does it look like I'm doing? I'm helping."

"What's the catch? What do you stand to gain from this? Am I missing something?" My head pulls back, and my brows slam together.

"Believe it or not, I can be nice."

"Highly doubtful."

"I know I'm a lawyer, but I'm sure I can work your

register and box up goodies so long as you don't mind me taking the occasional sample. Come on, Sweets." He flashes me a toothy grin that I immediately want to slap off his stupidly handsome face. "Let me help you."

I scoff, not knowing what else to do or sure how to respond to his proposition.

The last time he tried to 'help' I ended up with no boyfriend and an intact hymen. Nash has never been anything but a complete asshole manwhore his entire adult life. I'm not sure what bothers me more, him sleeping his way through Denver, bringing his whore-devours back to flaunt them through town, or being a dick to me at every turn.

Before I protest, he's pushing me toward the back, greeting the customers that trickled in and starting to take orders. Well. He's surprisingly competent. I consider staying up front, but Nash seems to have things under control, and I do have a shit-ton of work to do in the back. As much as I love this place, I don't want to spend the entire weekend before Christmas in it. It's not like I'd be far away. He can easily find me if he runs into trouble.

I spend the next several hours decorating and boxing up my custom cake orders. Every now and then Nash appears in the back, asking for a cake or more treats to fill the display. He's been a life saver. I still don't know what to think. He's an ass, then he's downright helpful. It's got my head spinning around like a dreidel. He hasn't said one snarky thing the entire time he's been here.

Chapter 4

If it wasn't for him, I'd have been here for hours after closing to get everything done. But now I'm lost. What do I do now? A thank you doesn't seem like enough. A hug is too much. I've made a point to never touch Nash. Putting my hands on him inevitably puts dirty thoughts in my head, and there's no way I'll ever willingly go there.

I walk back out to the front with the cheesecakes for Nash's mom and my last cake order. After placing them behind the counter, I lean against the doorway to watch him work. He does look nice in a pink apron; I'll give him that.

"Thank you, Sarah. You have a good day." He winks at Ms. Cole, our old high school math teacher, as he hands her a box of cupcakes. She blushes, tucking her chin down in her puffy winter jacket, before leaving. He turns around and gives me a lazy smile.

I push off the doorframe and take a tentative step toward him. "Mrs. James will be in for her cake. That's my last customer for the day." I give Nash a long look, searching his face for anything that may indicate he's here under false pretenses. I shake my head, finding none. "I don't know why you're helping me, but I appreciate it. Thank you, Nash."

"You can thank me with anything that's left in the case. I'll be my mom's hero if I bring anything else of yours to the Christmas Eve party. She's always going on about how she loves this place, and she may have mentioned getting something to go with the cheesecakes."

"I'll do you one better." I grab a box and fill it with the remaining cookies and brownies. "You and Sebastian can have these, and I'll make something for your mom in the morning, so it'll be fresh."

He grabs the box from me, shoving a chocolate chip cookie in his mouth. He moans as he chews. Does he make sounds like that when he eats other things? Dammit. Him being nice is frying my brain.

"But don't think this means we're friends. I still don't like you." I give him a sideways glance.

"I wouldn't dream of it. I don't like you either."

"Good."

"Good." He grins.

My eyes narrow on his smug face and before I can open my mouth for a good insult, the door chimes.

"Hello," Mrs. James calls out with a wave. "Merry Christmas, Julia."

"Merry Christmas. Perfect timing, I just boxed up your cake." I stand straight, force a smile, and speak with my most polite customer service voice.

Mrs. James eyes Nash speculatively. "Who's your helper? He sure is handsome."

Nash's deep laugh has tingles shooting up and down my spine. I shift and stretch out my legs. Must have been a long day on my feet.

"He thinks he is." Although I might agree, I'll never admit it out loud. "Did Weston make it home?"

"He did, but I'm afraid we're going to have to eat this marvelous cake without him." Her eyes brighten and the expression on her face tells me she's up to no good. "He's stuck up on the mountain with Cami. Sounds like they might be spending Christmas together."

My hand flies to my mouth and I let out a mocked gasp while Nash chuckles behind me. "I know you would never meddle and send him up there on purpose."

"I would never do that." The wiggling of her eyebrows says otherwise.

"Well, good luck to you." I come out from behind the counter and carefully hand her the cake. "I'll be rooting for them."

West and I didn't know each other well in high school, but I knew how hard it was for Cami to be left behind when he moved away. Them being stuck together would either end with a long overdue reconciliation or a fucking disaster.

"Well, you two enjoy yourselves." Mrs. James sends me a wink before settling her gaze on Nash. "She's a good one. If you're lucky enough to get her, don't be stupid enough to let her go."

"I wouldn't dream of it." Nash looks affronted, like he'd never think to let me go. He can keep dreaming. He'll never get me in the first place.

I roll my eyes as soon as Mrs. James is out the door. "I wouldn't dream of it." I mimic him, changing my voice to a deep timbre. I roll my eyes a second time. "You're such an ass."

"I've been told I have a nice ass." Nash pulls the apron from his neck and hangs it on one of the wall hooks. "Women always have nice things to say about me. Except for you."

"Maybe to your face. I'm sure they have plenty to say behind your back."

"More than likely. But since I only see them once, I really don't care."

I snap my mouth shut, turn to walk away, but whirl back to him. "Once is probably enough. I bet it's not worth it to come back a second time. Who wants to be disappointed twice?"

Nash shrugs. My disapproval over his love 'em and leave 'em attitude never bothered him before, and I'm sure it doesn't now. He claims he doesn't have time for a proper relationship, and that's why he never indulged in them. I figure it's because he's spineless and has a pencil dick.

And I don't see that changing anytime soon. Spines don't grow overnight, and pencil dicks are forever.

While I appreciate Nash's help today, and will make something delicious for his mom to make up for it, I need to get away from him. Or, at the very least, need a buffer. The longer I stay around Nash, the more I want to inflict him with violence.

"Sebastian's probably bored out of his mind. You can head on out."

"Why?" He pretends to look hurt. "You don't want to be alone with me?"

"No."

It's clear he's not leaving without me, the jerk, so I start turning out the lights.

He chuckles. "What happened to that boyfriend of yours? What's his name? Clark? Chris? Cain?"

"Cannon. He fell into my friend's vagina a few months ago."

"Ouch." He flinches, leading the way out of the shop. "You can't recover from that."

I flick the final light switch and lock up behind us. "Nope."

"No one since then?"

That's an odd question. Since when is he interested in my love life? He never asked or showed any interest before. He must be exhausted from putting in a day's worth of work that didn't involve sitting behind a desk.

"Look, Nash." I narrow my eyes on him. "I don't think it's any of your damn business who I date or don't date. Don't pretend like this little Christmas visit means you're involved with my life in any way. You're my brother's friend. Not mine."

"Noted." He clenches his jaw, prompting a tic as he inclines his head toward his car. "Let's go. I'm driving."

I push past him. "Good for you. I'm driving myself. I'll be back to the house shortly. Toodles."

I raise my hand and wiggle my fingers back and forth in a casual wave. I contemplate giving him the finger, but since I'm still in front of my shop, I need to keep some level of professionalism. Such a shame.

I keep walking down the sidewalk toward my car without so much as a backward glance. Lucky me, I have a nice pair of ass hugging jeans on, and I make sure to walk with an extra swish in my hips. There's no doubt in my mind this ladies' man is watching me make my way down the sidewalk. Welcome to the show. He's not the only one around here with a nice ass, and I'm not afraid to use mine to my advantage.

A smile stretches across my face as Nash's low rumbling laugh follows me to my car, confirming he is, in fact, watching my every move.

5

NASH

※

Jules is the biggest pain in the ass. The ass she swished all the way to the car when she knew damn well I was watching. I spend the entire drive back to her place thinking about shriveled old ladies, baseball diamonds, the spot of bird shit on my windshield. Anything and everything to get my dick soft before I face Bash. I don't need him thinking I'm coming home with a boner after spending time with his sister. Even if that's exactly the case.

Despite the ass distraction giving her a head start, I'm still able to beat Jules to the house. It looks like she drove a different way. Which is perfect, because I have no idea if Bash has got all the Christmas tree stuff up from the basement. There was so much of it, I'm probably an asshole for leaving him to do it alone. Between the four trees and all the other crap she has, I bet there's enough holiday decor to cover the entire house from *Home Alone*.

"Hey baby, I got us some cookies," I call out to Bash in a sing-songy voice as I swing open the front door.

"More cookies?" His face appears from behind the naked Christmas tree set up to the right of the fireplace, a broad smile spreading across his face. "Didn't think I'd put on ten pounds this holiday." He holds his stomach.

I chuckle. I'm figuring out Bash is his best self when he has a continuous supply of cookies. "Yeah. More cookies. Do you still need some help in the basement, or did you manage to haul everything up yourself?"

"I think I've got everything." Bash steps out from behind the tree, wiping a few stray pine needles from his shirt. "Whatever I'm missing, I figure you can get later. I also ordered dinner. Should be here in thirty. You're welcome."

I reach out and pat him on the shoulder as I walk by and head to the kitchen. "You're going to make a good wife one day."

"Fuck off. Give me the damn cookies."

"You're going to ruin your appetite." I tsk and give him my best imitation of my mom's disapproving stare. The one that usually comes out when she asks me about marriage and kids. She's been ready for grandkids like yesterday, and I don't want them ever. No woman has made me change my mind yet, and as long as they continue to be disposable, I'm not sure one ever will.

He blindly reaches into the box, pulls out a cookie at

random, and shoves it in his mouth whole. Such a charmer, this one. "Worth it."

The front door slams shut, and Bash and I both freeze in place, waiting to see what kind of reaction we'll get from this Christmas ambush.

"Hey, guys. What is all this? What's going on?"

Good news, she sounds confused, which is way better than pissed. As much as I like to poke the bear, I'm not trying to piss her off with this. Not when it involves the memory of her parents.

Bash's shoulders relax and he blows out a loud breath before turning around and gesturing toward the tree with an outstretched hand. "Surprise."

Her brows furrow as she looks at the tree and back at us. "I see that. We usually don't put up a tree."

"Well, *usually* we do." Bash's gaze falls to the ground, and he shuffles his feet. "At least we did before the accident. I know it's hard, but I want to have Christmas again. A real Christmas. With you."

Jules nods, her eyes tearing up, but she quickly swipes them away with the back of her hand. "I think I'd like that. Maybe we can start some new traditions?"

Oh, bad idea. I'm not ready to dress up as an elf and prance around for pictures. I mean, physically I can do it, but mentally, I don't think I have it in me.

"Absolutely." Bash tosses the box of cookies on the kitchen table and makes his way over to the tree. "Mom and Dad would want us to celebrate. And they always loved your ideas."

"No, they always *indulged* my ideas."

She's absolutely right. No one, and I mean no one

who's sane, would like her ideas. "That's correct, some of them were just awful."

Jules laughs and meets my gaze. Her lips curl in a smile and she mouths 'thank you.' With a brisk nod, I take a step back and let them dig through the boxes to find the lights and ornaments. There's a lightness to Jules that wasn't there earlier, even when she was waving her ass at me. As for me, I'm content sitting here watching them decorate the tree; it's not anything I need to be a part of.

The doorbell rings as Bash pulls out several strands of tangled white lights. He tosses them at Jules before heading to the door. "I'll get it. I ordered dinner."

"Come on, Nash. Help me with the lights." Jules smiles and curls her finger, beckoning me to her. That slender finger of hers is dangerous. She could beckon me anywhere with that thing. Like straight to hell if I'm not careful.

"Are you sure you don't want to wait for Bash?"

"I asked you, didn't I?"

Indeed, she did. Who am I to keep the lady waiting?

"I'll unwind and you can start wrapping. I can't reach the top."

I grab the lights out of Jules' outstretched hand and nudge her out of the way with my hip. "That's because you're a midget."

"Yeah, well." She cocks her head to the side and looks me up and down. "We can't all be six foot two giants."

I chuckle. I'm sure I am a giant to her. She barely comes to my shoulders. I can't complain. It makes me feel big, manly. After plugging in a strand to test the lights, I string them around the base of the tree, winding my way around it. Jules follows me closely, uncoiling the lights as I drape them among the branches, and adjusting where she's not happy with my positioning. She could do this herself, but I guess it's more fun to go behind me and 'fix' what I'm doing.

"So, am I correct to assume I have you to thank for all this?" She peers up at me, the soft glow of the Christmas lights illuminating her face. She looks fucking beautiful.

I turn my head back to the tree, desperately needing a distraction, and fiddle with the lights. I don't need to look at her like she's my last meal. "I may have mentioned a few things to Bash. He would have gotten there eventually."

She lays a hand lightly on my shoulder and gives it a squeeze. "You're giving him way too much credit. He's not the most observant."

"Maybe. You're important to him, Jules."

The flecks of gold in her light brown eyes are striking in the bright white lights from the tree. She's important to me. I wish I could tell her how I really feel. How I want her to be mine, even if it's only for one night. But fuck, my hands, and tongue are bound to her brother's promise.

Jules holds my gaze, a slight dusting of pink on her cheeks. "Thanks, Nash."

"Of course."

"But don't read into any of this," Jules blurts, breaking whatever moment we shared. "Decorating for

Christmas makes me nice. I'll go back to hating you tomorrow."

"Alright, assholes." Bash comes back into the living room, and I take a quick step away from Jules. "I've got the Chinese in the microwave to keep it warm. Let's finish up with these lights so we can eat."

Jules gives him a patronizing glare and gestures toward the kitchen. "If you want to eat, go ahead. Nash and I have the lights."

"Nonsense." Bash narrows his eyes at me before raising his brows in question. I'm sure we'll be having a conversation about this later. "I'll just turn on the Christmas music. We could stand to be a bit more festive around here."

While Bash queues up a Christmas playlist I'm sure contains more Mariah Carey than any man should listen to, I turn back to Jules. She's working on a particularly nasty tangle, but her eyes keep glancing my way. Small furtive looks that have me wondering if maybe she doesn't hate me as much as she thinks she does.

If that's the case, we're in trouble. Her hatred is the only thing holding me at bay. The only thing that keeps my hands to myself and my promise to Bash intact. I need to be a good friend, a loyal friend.

But I may need her more.

6

JULES

❄

What the hell's wrong with me?

I'm supposed to hate Nash. I do hate Nash. Just because he does something super sweet and selfless, like talking my brother into renewing our Christmas traditions or helping out at the bakery, doesn't mean all's forgiven. He's still a manwhore with no respect for women. Or me. And he's still the man who destroyed my first love for no damn reason.

Even though I hate to admit, it softens a spot in my hardened heart. But that's it. No more feelings toward Nash.

His good deed yesterday has nothing to do with the truffles I'm making for his mom's Christmas Eve party. They're for her because she's a lovely woman, whom I happen to be fond of. Unlike her son. Who's infuriatingly altruistic and irritatingly handsome.

As if he can hear my thoughts, Nash strolls into the

kitchen in a pair of gray sweats and a white t-shirt, sipping the cup of coffee he stole from the kitchen earlier. Those gray sweats are like catnip for women and I'm not immune. I desperately need someone to burn them or make them illegal. The way they cling to his bulge… His impressive looking bulge… Dammit.

Eyes on the chocolate Rowe. Eyes on the freaking chocolate.

"What are you doing up so early?"

I spin around with a corner of my lips tipped up in a half smile. "Dipping your balls in chocolate."

Would have been a funnier joke if I wasn't eyeballing his crotch again.

"That would be a first for me, but I'm open to trying new things." Nash leans his ass against the counter and takes a sip of his coffee.

"I'll absolutely cut them off for you if you want. If you wish to present those balls to your mom at her party tonight, by all means, pull them out. I'll get the kitchen scissors."

Sebastian chooses that moment to walk into the kitchen and press a quick kiss to my temple. "Good morning. What exactly are we pulling out and cutting off?"

"Your danglers if you want to serve them at the party tonight. I'm dipping balls." I arch a brow and focus on a wide-eyed Sebastian before my eyes land on Nash, who's appropriately choking on his coffee. "No takers?"

Sebastian takes a quick step away, his face twisted in disgust, like I was talking about my period. "I'm sorry I asked. There's no instance I can think of where I would want to show my balls to Nash's mom."

"I'm sure she'd love to see your balls, especially if they're festive." Nash grins wickedly.

Sebastian groans before running a hand down his face. "I think your dad may disagree."

I dip another gingerbread truffle in the melted chocolate, swirling it around to make sure it's completely covered. "So, we're done talking about your balls. No one needs to see them. What are your plans for the day? Are you both heading over for the party early?"

"We're going early, but not for a while." Sebastian pours himself a cup of coffee from the pot I made earlier. "We've got plenty of time to bother you while you're fondling balls."

"Oh joy. I'm so excited."

"What can we do to help?" Sebastian comes up beside me, grabs one of the freshly dipped balls and throws it in his mouth. A mouth that pops open, and he fans frantically. "It's hot."

Nash flanks my other side. "No shit, dummy. It's melted chocolate. It's supposed to be hot."

"If you guys want to help." I elbow Nash with a grunt when he comes too far into my bubble. "I've got a white chocolate drizzle in that little squirt bottle. One of you can put that on top of the dried truffles."

Both guys wear identical looks of confusion, mouths slightly agape, brows knitted together, and heads tilted to the right. Apparently, they can dazzle in the courtroom with their fancy lawyer talk, but something as simple as drizzling chocolate stumps them.

"Well." I push away from the counter, grab the bottle, and demonstrate the back-and-forth motion of a drizzle with a few of the truffles. "Easy peasy guys. Surely two brainiacs such as yourselves can figure this out."

Smash and Bash look at each other, nodding in a silent conversation I'm not privy to. I ignore them, like I usually do, and head back to my ball dipping.

Nash sighs and grabs the bottle out of Sebastian's hands. "Fine. I'll do it. Your meaty paws would only fuck it up, anyways."

"It's true. These hands aren't made for delicate precision work. Yours are much more feminine."

"Fuck you."

"Only in your wildest dreams, lover boy."

I roll my eyes. These guys are a couple of idiots. They could've had the truffles finished by now. After a little groaning and moaning, Nash gets to work. His drizzle is surprisingly good. I mean, not as good as mine, but almost professional looking.

Almost.

With my dipping, Nash's finishing touches, and Sebastian's supervision, we're finished in no time. This'll give me some time to relax before getting ready for the party tonight.

"Well, thanks, guys. I've got cleanup covered. Why don't you two go play video games or play in traffic or something?"

Chapter 6

My brother looks over at me, his brows raised. "We're lawyers. We don't play in traffic."

"And the video games."

"Might not be a bad idea. Nash, you're about to get your ass handed to you."

Finally, they leave, and just when I get the kitchen cleaned up my phone rings. I peer down at the screen to see a picture of Holly, my best friend since high school.

I answer after a few rings. "Hey, Holly. How's it going?"

"Hey girl," Holly's voice sounds through the phone. "I have some good news for you."

"Oh? I'm intrigued."

She laughs. It's not an innocent laugh, mind you. It's the one that says there's a high probability she's up to no good. "Nick Stratton will be at the party tonight. He's been single for a couple weeks now. I just so happened to run into him at the store earlier today and he asked about you."

There it is. Holly's been trying to set me up with Nick for months. He's nice, handsome, successful, but our timing never lined up. I was dating Cannon the Vagina Slayer and then Nick started dating an out-of-towner.

"And Vince told me he mentioned you at his last cleaning. You could do worse, landing the town dentist."

I laugh. "You know I don't care about that shit. But I'll make sure to look for him tonight. I could use a conversation with a nice guy for once."

"Nice guy? Has Cannon called you?" Holly hisses through the phone. "I will cut off that man's dick."

"No. No. Nothing like that." I lower my voice in case Nash or Sebastian try to eavesdrop. "Sebastian invited Nash to come stay with us. At my freaking house. He's been an ass per usual, but he's also been a little nice. I don't know how to deal. He's giving me whiplash."

"Nice? What do you mean nice? He's never nice."

"Right? He stopped by the shop. He actually came in to torment me. I saw it written all over his stupid face. But after he saw how busy I was, he turned into some white knight and jumped behind the counter to help me out."

"What?" she squeals. "That's crazy."

I throw my free hand out in front of me, gesturing wildly. "I know, right? He's never tried to help before. And he talked Sebastian into helping me decorate for Christmas."

"It sounds like he's definitely being more than nice." She pauses. "Is he still as good looking as he was last time I saw him?"

"He's not good looking," I lie quickly. Maybe a little too quickly.

"No? Not even a little?" She sounds skeptical, even over the phone. "You know I'll see him tonight."

I huff. Holly always knows when I'm lying. It's really inconvenient. "I don't know, Holly. What do you want me to say here? That he's smoking hot? That he was cute back when we were teenagers, and now that he's a filled-out man, he's fucking sexy? Is that what you want to know?"

"Just wanted you to admit it. Not really to me, but to yourself."

"Yeah, thanks for that. I could have done without it."

"Well, that's too damn bad." Holly hums through the phone as if to say 'told you so.' "I've seen you two together. I think you're both attracted to each other, but neither one of you will admit it."

"You're too much. And you're also wrong. Nash and I aren't into each other. We despise each other. Always have. We tolerate each other because of Sebastian."

She laughs. "No, you haven't fucked each other silly because of Sebastian. There's a fine line between love and hate, Jules, and you two have been walking that line for years."

I scoff. She's way off base. She's so far off base, she's in a different field. Yeah, Nash is hot. I can admit that. But that's it. There's no attraction, no fleeting lust, no reaction other than hatred.

"Stuff it, Holly. Take this as a victory, I'm going to talk to Nick tonight. Maybe he can be my Christmas present from Santa. And there will be no more talk of Nash."

There might be a fine line between love and hate, but with all the history between Nash and me, there's no chance I'll ever cross it.

Not in a million years.

7

NASH

❄

My hair is tousled to perfection, and I've got on my favorite lady killing, ass hugging pants. But nothing, and I mean nothing, can detract from the giant cat face sweater with a sewn in scarf and bells. I didn't even ask my mom where she got this hideous thing. I don't want to know. That would mean there's more of them. Thankfully, Bash is in something equally hideous. His has a Christmas tree on the front, also with stylish bells, and lights that work.

You know, just in case the bells aren't enough to draw attention.

Jules is in a black sweater dress thing with white and red snowflakes, and she looks adorable in her distractingly fitted leggings that reveal every curve of her mouthwatering legs. Unfortunately, I'm not the only one that notices.

My blood simmers and I take some deep breaths to

calm myself. Almost every guy here has turned his head in her direction at least once. Even those married fuckers. I've got to get myself under control before I end up beating the shit out of one of them. I'm sure that would go over as well as it did ten years ago.

Like a lead balloon.

I grab a glass of red wine from the bartender my mom hired and toss it back before grabbing another. I glance at Jules and frown at her chatting in a small group with another girl and two guys. One of them seems particularly engaged with her, and it pisses me off even more.

"Hey there. I like your pussy cat." The feminine phone sex operator voice pulls my attention away from Jules.

Holy big boobs. Her black dress is low cut and skintight, contrasting her tanned skin and platinum hair. I don't think she got the memo about wearing an ugly sweater, or any kind of sweater, but no one seems to mind. It doesn't hurt her case that it's a tad bit nipply in here.

"Hi." I know it's not the wittiest greeting, but between Jules talking to strange men and this woman's large rack, I'm distracted.

"I'm Cali." She peers up at me, bats her fake eyelashes, and smiles. To add to the effect, as if it wasn't obvious enough she wants my attention, she twists a piece of hair around her index finger. "And you know, that sweater would look great on my bedroom floor."

If she looks like a hooker, talks like a hooker, and is named like a hooker, well, she might be a hooker. I'm

Chapter 7

not sure if she's here on a night off or if I should ask her how much she charges for an hour.

"Nice to meet you, Cali." I tug on the frayed ends of the scarf sewn into my sweater, trying to think of how to remove myself from this conversation without being rude. "I'm—"

Cali flips her hair over her shoulder and giggles. "Oh, I know who you are, silly. You're one of the big-time lawyers from Denver."

"Yep, that's me." I give her a tight smile and drink down the rest of my wine before exchanging it for another glass. Between Jules and this conversation, I need all the wine I can get.

"What do you say we get out of here and get to know each other better?"

Jesus. This girl is forward. I like a little cat and mouse game, but she's serving herself up on a silver platter and I can't even *pretend* to be interested. Maybe it's the woman with the honey blonde hair narrowing her amber eyes at me from across the room while they flash in anger.

"Sorry, this is my mom's party. I actually need to go socialize. But my business partner is over there if you want to say hello to him. He actually owns most of the business, he's practically my boss," I lie through my teeth and point to Bash. Her eyes twinkle with little dollar signs as she walks off to intercept Sebastian.

I breathe out a sigh of relief. He can figure out how to get rid of her. Bash hates bimbos, so he'll more than likely punch me for sending her over, but that's a problem for a later time.

I turn back to Jules and catch her backside as she walks down one of the hallways off from the main room, hanging off the arm of one of the assholes she was talking to.

My nostrils flare and my blood boils as a wave of rage flows through my body. What the fuck is she doing go off with some d-bag? My body jolts with recognition as they disappear into the next room.

Nick Stratton. Hell no. He's more of a man slut than I am, which is saying something. Bash isn't going to like Jules going off to hook up with him. I've got to stop this shit. No one is going to touch her while I'm around.

Even me.

But especially not that jerkoff.

I drain my new glass, put it back on the bar with a little more force than necessary, and stomp my way across the room.

8

JULES

❄

"I'm glad I ran into you." Nick leans sideways against the wall, his arm raised and bent above his head, and grins at me.

"Me too." I nod, clasping my hands in front of me and twisting them. I should be concentrating on Nick, but I can't get the picture of that slutty woman with her hands on Nash out of my head. She obviously can't read. The invitation clearly said sweater, not whore dress that barely covers your tits and ass. "I know we've been trying to catch up with each other for a few months now and things never seem to line up."

He leans toward me and winks, but it's not one of those smooth winks. This guy winks with the whole side of his face. I used to think he was a pretty attractive guy, but maybe I never saw him up close. "With any luck, things will line up this time."

"For sure." Or wait? Is that a pickup line? Now, I'm

not sure and don't know what I just agreed to. Damn Nash for distracting me. Nick is supposed to be the distraction.

Nick reaches out and trails a finger down my arm. I'm sure it's supposed to elicit a reaction, but I feel nothing. It's like I'm completely dead inside. No belly flips. No lady tingles. Nada. Worst distraction ever. He does nothing to rid me of my Nash riddled thoughts.

"What do you think you're doing?" Nash's voice sounds over my shoulder. It's not loud, but the rage is clear.

Nick jumps back like he's been shocked, his hand falling to his side, and his eyes widening. Anger surges through me. Nash's song and dance routine is getting old. It was necessary at the bar, but this is too much. If I want to find someone for a hookup, that's my prerogative. I don't need a clam jam.

I spin around and glare at Nash. "I don't need your help, Nash. Nick and I are just talking."

"Like hell you are." Nash's jaw clenches and his hands fist at his sides.

"Nash," I hiss, fire flooding my veins. "What are you doing?"

"I need to talk to you," he grinds out through clenched teeth.

"Now? I'm kinda in the middle of something. We can talk later."

"No, we can talk now." Nash takes a step closer and dips his head to look me directly in the eyes.

I step forward, standing toe to toe with him. My stomach starts to flutter, and a shiver runs down my spine. Of course, my stupid body reacts to Nash and not Nick. Clearly, it hates me, but not Nash. Me and my libido need to have a heart to heart.

"Later."

Nash grunts and points over his shoulder. "Get the fuck out of here, Nick."

"Sorry, Jules. This isn't worth it," Nick mumbles as he edges past us and escapes back to the party.

"What is your—"

Before I can finish, Nash grabs my arm, spins me around and starts walking us farther into the room. I struggle and try to pull away, but Nash's grip tightens.

"What's wrong with you?" I slap at his hand. "Let go of me."

Nash keeps his lips pressed in a flat line until he propels us into a bedroom, flips on the light, and slams the door shut behind us. "I told you I need to talk to you."

"Yeah, I got that part." I prop my hands on my hips. "What the fuck is wrong with you?"

Nash runs a hand through his hair. "What are you doing talking to that guy?"

"Nick? Is that what this is about?"

"Yeah, Nick."

I tap my foot against the floor and stare him down, waiting for him to continue. I'm not going to spend my night arguing with him about, well, I don't even know. I'm not entirely sure what's going on. Is Nash jealous? But that's not right. Nash doesn't get jealous, and he sure as hell has no reason to be jealous where I'm concerned.

"The guy's scum, Julia. I hear about all the women he sleeps with, and I don't even live here. He just wants to fuck you and move on."

I throw my head back and laugh. "Isn't this the pot calling the kettle black? This is real rich coming from the likes of you."

"I know how it sounds. I'm looking out for you. You're not a one-night stand kind of girl."

"Oh, come on." I'm no stranger to the one-night horizontal mambo. It doesn't happen often, but sometimes no strings orgasms are better than spending the night alone. "How do you know what I am? Maybe I don't mind a one-night stand. I could use a good time. You're not my brother. I don't even know why you care."

His jaw tightens as he takes a step in my direction. "I don't care."

"Could have fooled me." I take a step forward, my eyes never leaving his. "Now, move. I'm going to go find Nick."

"Like fuck you are," Nash grits out before his lips crash into mine.

I stand momentarily stunned, blood pounding in my ears. I should be pushing him away, punching him in the face, anything that lets him know kissing me isn't okay. But instead, I run my hands over his chest, his hard muscles bunching under my hands, and kiss him back with everything I have. The fluttering in my stomach is back, going crazy. I curl my fingers in his ugly ass sweater, the bells dinging, and I pull him closer.

Nash torments me with gentle bites and teasing

flicks of his tongue before kissing me hard enough to bruise. He threads a hand through my hair and tugs my head back as he runs his tongue along the seam of my lips. His spicy aftershave is intoxicating, and he tastes like a fruity red wine. Delicious.

With a small moan, I open up to him. Nash sweeps his tongue into my mouth, gliding it along mine. Teasing me. Tasting me. *Oh, fuck. Since when did kissing get this good?*

A groan vibrates his chest, and his other hand squeezes my ass, grinding me into his growing erection. Even at half mast, I can tell it's as impressive as it looked in those damn sweatpants. My clit throbs, needing attention, needing that dick in Nash's pants, and I grind against it.

Abruptly, Nash releases me and takes a step back. My hands fall back to my sides as we stare at each other, both of us breathing heavily.

"I'm so sorry." Nash starts to reach out to me but clenches his fist halfway and shoves it in his pocket instead. "I shouldn't have done that."

I run my tongue along my bottom lip, tasting the lingering flavor of wine from Nash's mouth. I stare at him, not sure what to say, and an awkward silence hangs between us. "I'm not sure what to do here."

"There's nothing to do." Nash takes a step back. "I just—I need to get back to the party. I'm sorry."

I don't even know what to say. Do I want him to go? To stay? I don't get a choice, though. Nash spins around and runs from the room, his bells jingling all the way back to the party.

I brush my fingers along my lips. His kiss was the best damn kiss of my life. And I don't know how to process what the hell just happened. I don't like Nash; I don't want to like Nash.

God, but my body wants him. He lit me up like the Christmas tree he talked Sebastian into setting up for me. I groan at the reminder. Sebastian.

He'll pummel Nash if he finds out he kissed me. It's a guarantee to ruin Christmas. Which is why Sebastian can't find out about that kiss and why it can never happen again.

9

NASH

❄

I KISSED HER. I fucking kissed her. What was I thinking? Oh, wait, I wasn't thinking. My dick was. And maybe my primal caveman side, too. Bash will lose his fucking mind, and as shitty as it is, there's no way I can tell him a thing. Not when I lost myself in a kiss with his sister that could move fucking mountains, violating the one and only promise I made to him.

Now, I'm going to have to look him in the face and lie to him. Lie to the one man who's like a brother to me.

"Hey, lover." Bash comes up behind me and claps me on the shoulder. "Thanks for fucking me."

I flinch. My body stiffens, my heart sputters and my palms sweat. I wasn't even this nervous my first day in the courtroom. "I'm so sorry, Bash, I—"

"It's fine." Bash waves me off. "I got rid of her

pretty easily. All I had to point out was my mom's doctor friend, and she was off."

I breathe out a sigh of relief. I'd completely forgotten about Cali. I'm such an idiot, there's no way he knows about Jules. Fuck my life.

"I think there's a good chance she's some kind of hooker or escort."

Bash laughs. "I think you're probably right. I got that vibe as soon as she opened her mouth. Do you think we've been here long enough? I'm ready to get home and out of this ridiculous sweater. I don't know where your mom found these, but they should be burned. And look at yours." He pauses and jingles the bells on my sweater with a shit-eating grin. "That's the scariest thing I've ever seen. She's right about one thing, though."

"Oh yeah? What's that?"

"You're a pussy."

I push Bash, causing him to take a step back. "Fuck you. And yes, I think we can leave. Go find Jules. I'm going to say goodbye to Mom, and I'll meet you at the car."

My gut clenches as I say her name. I can only pray to any God that may listen, she won't utter a word to Bash. With a slight shake of my head to regain my senses, I head off to kiss Mom goodbye and drag myself to the car, preparing for the most awkward trip in the history of trips.

Jules eyes me from the backseat as I open the passenger door and sit down. Keeping my eyes forward, I buckle up and fold my hands in my lap. *Don't mind me, just minding my own business here.*

"Well, that was fun. I don't know about you all, but I'm ready to get out of this damn sweater." Sebastian glances to the rear-view mirror, presumably at Jules. "Where were you earlier? I ran into Mrs. Jones, mom's old best friend, and she was asking about you."

I take a deep breath and hold it, praying for the first time in a long time. She either lies for me or I'm about to get my ass kicked in a hideous jingling cat sweater. I'm hoping she covers for me. I'm not ready to lose my best friend and business partner.

"Holly wanted to talk to me about her and Vince. There was a misunderstanding. He pushed things way too far and didn't even stick around to talk to her about it. It was a real dick move."

Holy shit. I really thought she was going to out me. My shoulders sag with relief, and I can finally breathe easy. Yeah, it was a dick move, but I most assuredly took things too far. I didn't know what to say, still don't. I can't admit everything, and I certainly can't let it happen again. There's no coming back from that kiss.

But I want to. I want to keep kissing her until she doesn't remember her own name.

I'll never be able to look at her without picturing my tongue in her mouth and her plump ass in my hands.

Fuck. I'm so screwed.

"Sounds like it," Sebastian rumbles.

As soon as we get back to her place, I mumble something about being tired and flee upstairs to my room like the fucking coward I am. I take off the ugliest sweater ever made, think twice about throwing it in the fireplace, and change into a pair of black joggers and a white t-shirt before throwing myself on the bed.

I toss and turn for what feels like hours. All I can think about is how Jules opened up to me. How my tongue glided against hers, exploring the softness of her mouth. How fucking sweet she tasted. I bet if I explored lower, I'd find her wet and aching for me.

I flip over on my back, my cock turning to steel, and I palm my length through the fabric of the joggers. Jules' hand would feel so much better wrapped around me, pumping up and down, putting her knee on either side of my hips and taking me into her body.

Touching her is a line I swore I'd never cross, but the fact that I did tonight, breaking my promise to Bash, deflates my dick slightly. I groan, sitting up and swinging my legs off the side of the bed. I'm sure now she won't even talk to me. Not after I ran out of the room like an asshole. I should get up and apologize, let her know it was my fault. Maybe I can convince her never to breathe a word of it to Sebastian. She may have covered my ass earlier, but it doesn't mean she'll keep doing it.

Talking to her, smoothing things over, is the right thing to do.

With a grunt, I push myself up from the bed, and make my way into the hallway. Squinting in the dim light of a nightlight, I shuffle my way along the corridor. Turning on the lights, although convenient, might wake up Bash. And I can't explain why I'm up so late walking in the direction of his sister's room with a chubby.

I stop in my tracks as a petite shadow approaches

me from the other end of the hall. What the hell's she doing out here? And why is *she* sneaking around in the dark?

"Jules?" I lower my voice to a whisper.

"Nash?" she whispers back, stopping in front of me, her hands twisting around in front of her.

"Jules, I…" I gaze down into her amber eyes, their color bright, despite the muted light.

Face to face with Jules, I don't know what to say. I thought I had everything worked out, but here I am standing in front of her with absolutely nothing coming out of my mouth. Shit. Maybe this was a mistake. Maybe I should turn tail and run back to my room.

My chest heaves as I struggle to breathe, and my heart pounds. Jules' eyes move back and forth between mine and my lips, and I know for sure I should turn around. This is heading straight for trouble, but I can't find it in me to move. I'm completely rooted in place, hovering on the edge of her essence, dying for a taste.

I reach out to place a hand on her half-covered shoulder, longing to touch her bare flesh, but change my mind halfway and let it fall back to my side. I don't deserve to lay a hand on her. It'll be better for the both of us if I turn around and walk away.

Closing my eyes, I start to do just that but Jules' hands on my bicep stops me. Her eyes search mine. My mouth goes dry, my body buzzing with energy, and my stomach flips.

"Fuck it," she mumbles before lurching up on her toes and sealing her lips to mine in a delicious kiss.

Shock waves ripple down my spine and my balls tighten.

I groan against the soft flesh of her mouth, wrapping my hands around her waist before running my palms over her ass, and pulling her to me. Her soft body molds to mine, and I love how she fits against me. My tongue dives past the seam of her lips into the wet, velvety warmth of her mouth. Right into heaven.

Now that I've got my hands on her, there's no way I can walk away. Not without knowing what she looks like when she comes undone by my hand, how her body tastes, and what makes her scream.

Although, we're going to have to muffle those.

10

JULES

❄

This is crazy, nuts, insane, and nothing has ever felt more right. My rational side is holding up stop signs and blinking warning lights, while my orgasm needing side wants more. More of Nash. More of his hands, more of his mouth, and absolutely more of that cock in his pants.

Nothing's forgiven and him and I are still far from okay, but I need to get this out of my system. Maybe then I'll be able to move on. He hasn't left my thoughts since he kissed me earlier. He only does one-night stands, and that's perfect because that's all I'm going to give him.

In.

Out.

No one has to know.

Especially Sebastian.

My hands glide up his back, and his arms slither

around my waist as he guides me into my bedroom. With the bottom of my foot, I push the door closed behind me, careful to shut it quietly. His muscles flex under my hands as I smooth them under his shirt, running my fingers along the ridges of his abs and over his pecs.

I tear myself away from him long enough to pull his t-shirt over his head and toss it to the floor. I want to look at him, admire his muscular body, but I want his mouth on mine more. My hands plunge in his hair, pulling him down to me while he circles my hips with his hands and inches up my tank top. His fingers are soft on my skin, and I long to feel them everywhere.

A shiver runs down my spine, the walls of my pussy clench, and lust shoots through my veins. My nipples peak, ready for his fingers, and my clit aches for attention. Fuck me. I know this puts me on the naughty list, but I can't fucking stop. Not until we both have a very merry Christmas.

His tongue explores my mouth, rolling against mine, as his fingers dance up my stomach, skirting around the underside of my breasts and flicking across my nipples. My stomach dips and I groan into his mouth. He pinches my tightened buds and rolls them between his fingers, dancing right on that edge between pleasure and pain. I love that line. He increases the pressure, and I can't help but whimper. It hurts so good. So fucking good.

Nash pulls back, dragging my lower lip between his teeth before trailing his tongue down my neck. "Fuck

Chapter 10

me, Jules. I don't deserve you, but I've gotta have you. Bash can't know. For either of our sakes."

"I know." I plunge a hand down the front of his pants, grab hold of his thick erection, and bite back a moan. His dick feels so velvety hard, and I swipe my thumb across the pre-cum on his tip. "I'll be quiet. Tonight never happened."

My tank top joins his shirt on the floor, and Nash palms my breast and lowers his head to my chest. He circles around my nipple with his tongue before sucking it into his mouth and catching it between his teeth. He nibbles and licks. I'm on the verge of orgasm and he's barely touched me. Using the hand that's not pumping his dick, I guide him to my other breast. Can't have it left out.

"You're a greedy little thing. Don't worry, Sweets, I'm going to make sure this is one of the best nights you've ever had."

Holy hell.

He pushes me down to the bed and rips off my pink checkered pajama pants. I let my legs fall open, exposing myself to him fully. Nash's eyes roam over me, taking me in, and he licks his lips. He crawls into the space between my legs, eying me like he's starved and I'm dinner.

Nash pushes my legs open wider and attacks my pussy. The man unleashes a full assault on my clit, sucking it into his mouth, raking his teeth across it and flicking it with his tongue. I reach out to grab a pillow and hold it over my face to muffle my cries. I'm not exactly quiet, and he's pushing every one of my buttons.

Every.

Single.

One.

He doesn't waste time with small tugs and light teases. No. Nash is all in with hard tugs of suction and firm pressure against my clit. He's revved me from zero to sixty in seconds. I'm about to detonate, and he's just getting started. My back arches and my hips buck against him as I push the pillow harder against my mouth, muffling my moans and whimpers.

Nash's mouth is fucking magic, and I chant his name into the pillow. We haven't even fucked, and I'm ruined.

I have no shame as I grind my pussy against his mouth. He plunges a finger inside me, and my body tightens around him as he fucks me, slowly dragging that thick digit in and out. I move my hips up, chasing his finger as he pulls it out of my wet heat. Before I can protest, there's pressure against my back hole.

My body tenses. I've never had a guy stick his finger in my ass before, but the thought sends a shiver of anticipation through me. I will myself to relax as his moistened finger circles my back entrance and pushes inside. I grip the pillow at the flash of pain as he penetrates that tight muscular ring. My ass clenches at the invasion, and I unleash a long-muffled groan. He fills me in a way that's so dirty, yet I crave more. I love that delicious burn and rock my hips to force him to move.

He draws that finger back, slowly, torturously, before pushing back in. I move up and down, meeting his strokes as he continues his slow rhythm. A low rumble rolls out of him, and he finally starts to fuck my ass with his finger, plunging it in and out of me with abandon while his tongue presses down on my clit, kneading it ruthlessly.

I'm grasping for control over my body, but I have none. My hips come off the bed and start to jerk, pleasure vibrates through me, turning me into a sexual tuning fork. I can't see, I can't breathe, I can't…I can't…an orgasm, more intense than anything I've ever had, rips through me. The waves of pleasure have me convulsing until I'm nothing but a limp, boneless body. I shove the pillow aside and struggle to catch my breath.

Nash slides his finger from my ass and peers up at me with a smirk. "I knew you weren't entirely sweet. You're just my kind of naughty." He crawls up my legs, leaving a trail of kisses. He hesitates, looking at me, his face contorted in a mix of lust and horror. "Please tell me you have a condom."

I fling my hand into the drawer of my nightstand, searching frantically, knocking crap to the floor until I grab a condom, and toss it in his direction. "Hurry."

"Bossy little thing."

I gaze up at the ceiling taking in a few deep breaths to calm my racing heart after that orgasm. I don't know how he expects me to forget that.

Nash kicks off his pants and rolls the condom over his erection. He falls over me, his arms braced on either side. "Are you ready?"

"God, yes." I lift my head and fuse my mouth with his, tasting myself on his lips.

His hips push forward, and he seats himself inside me before pulling almost all the way back. I arch into him, pressing my chest to his, and clutch at his shoulders. His cock presses against my walls and he advances slowly, giving me time to adjust around him. My eyelids flutter shut, relishing how completely he fills me. How good it feels. How right it is.

"Open your eyes. Look at me." His growled order has me staring into the stormy blue of his eyes. "I want you to know who's fucking you, Julia. Who gives you what you need."

Nash sinks into me, pressing me into the bed, plunging all the way inside, grinding his hips against mine. I try to move my body, to meet his stroke, but his weight keeps me pinned, letting me know he's in control.

I fucking love it.

His hand curls around one of my legs and brings it to his waist as his hips begin to drive into me. I forget about breathing. I forget my own damn name. I can only think about his cock and what it's doing to my body as he pistons into me hard and fast.

He's brutal. Devastating. Overwhelming.

My nails dig into the muscles of his shoulders as he slams into me, his eyes never leaving mine. I roll my lips together and clamp down, but the moans still escape my throat. Nash fastens a hand over my mouth, stifling me. The only sounds are the slap of flesh meeting flesh and our harsh panting as we struggle to breathe.

The walls of my pussy flutter and my legs quake. I arch against Nash as another orgasm rips through me, and I tighten around him. His chest rumbles and his movements become more erratic until his body jerks. He stills above me, his forehead resting on mine, as our panted breaths meet between us.

My heart rate returns to normal, and I lean forward, planting light, teasing kisses along the salty skin of his throat.

"Fuck, Julia." Nash leans forward, resting his head on my shoulder, his breathing still labored.

I drag my fingertips in light circles along his back before tracing up the column of his neck and sinking in his damn hair to muss it.

"Best Christmas present ever." Nash mumbles into my collarbone and presses his lips to my flesh for a delicate caress. "I can't move."

I give him a playful swat on the ass. "It wasn't exactly what I asked Santa for, but I'll take it."

With a chaste kiss on the lips, Nash pushes himself up and disappears into the bathroom. I roll on my side and pull the comforter up my body. I can't believe I just did that. With Nash. Actually, what I can't believe is how Nash was able to give me the two best orgasms of my life. How am I supposed to move on and forget this? And more importantly, what does this mean? I'm not ready to forgive him for what he's done to me, yet being with him felt more right than anything I'd ever known.

After a few minutes, he crawls under the covers and pulls my back against his front. He wraps his arms around me and lays a lingering kiss to my bare shoulder.

"What are you doing?" I whisper, even as my body relaxes into his. "I thought this was a one-time thing."

"It's a one-night thing. Santa only gets to come once a year, but I'm going to make sure we both come multiple times before his ass goes back to the North Pole."

I push against him, settling myself in his lap and weaving my hands through his, my body moving and adjusting to him on its own accord.

This is when I know, despite the merriment of Christmas Eve and the lingering holiday spirit, that I'm in trouble.

11

NASH

❄

A LOUD THUD startles me awake, I blink my eyes open and peer down at Jules. The pale light streaming in the window tells me I've overstayed my welcome, and I need to sneak back to my room. I nuzzle her shoulder blade before giving it a quick kiss.

"What the fuck are you doing?" Bash's voice crashes through my morning haze.

I roll away from Jules as fast as I can and push myself up from the bed, immediately taking a step back and putting my hands up in surrender. I can't believe I was so stupid to fall asleep in her bed. I've never fallen asleep with a woman before. I'd like to blame exhaustion from three vigorous rounds of sex, but really it's Jules. I didn't realize how much I'd love holding her while she slept. Being vulnerable to me. Trusting me.

"It's not what you think."

I realize how pathetic this sounds, but I have no

other excuse loaded up. Maybe he'll believe I mixed up bedrooms in the middle of the night.

Sebastian's eyes narrow on me and roam down my body before settling on my crotch. "Not what it looks like, huh? So, you didn't fuck my sister?"

A quick glance down tells me I'm sporting a full morning wood. In front of my best friend. Clearing up any confusion about the fact that I did fuck his sister last night. Could this possibly get any worse? I look around for something to cover my dick. Anything at this point would be nice. I'd even take that horrible cat sweater. Where the fuck are my clothes?

"Nash." Jules pulls my attention to her as she tosses me a pillow, which I use to hastily cover my shit. Her wide eyes move between Bash and me before she clutches the comforter to her breasts, but not before flashing us each a peek at her tightened pink nipples.

"Christ." Bash puts a hand up on the side of his face to block his view of Jules. "Put some fucking clothes on."

Fuck. Fuckity fuckity fuck. Yep, that makes it worse.

I'm pretty sure walking in on his best friend with a hard dick and his naked sister is Sebastian's worst nightmare. Maybe second worst nightmare. At least we weren't still fucking. He may be scarred for life.

"So, what's it going to be, *brother*? You couldn't find your room? You tripped and my sister cushioned your fall? You were both freezing to death and had to keep each other warm?" Bash cocks his head as he glares at me. His hands clenched into tight fists at his side and his nostrils flare. I've never seen him so pissed, and I can't say I blame him. In his eyes, I committed the biggest sin there is.

"It's my fault. This is on me. Come on, Sebastian," Jules pleads with him, but he refuses to take his eyes off me.

I shake my head. We all know who's to blame. "This isn't on you, Julia. I knew better. I made a promise to your brother, and I broke it."

"You're damn right you did." His tightens and his eyes flash in anger. "You broke a lot more than just some promise."

"What promise? What are you guys talking about?"

I sigh, running my free hand through my hair. Redemption. Finally, a chance to set things straight. To stop being the bad guy. To tell the truth for once. "I promised Nash ten years ago, I would never touch you."

"Ten years ago?" Her brows furrow in confusion.

I glance at Bash, who's shaking his head, telling me not to go there. Not to reveal the past. But I'm tired of being weighed down by this secret. It's time she knows everything.

"Colby Jenkins, your boyfriend you loved too much. I caught him with his tongue down some girl's throat."

Her eyes widen and she gasps. "You're lying. There's no way he would cheat on me. You beat the shit out of him because you didn't like him."

I hang my head and give it a slight shake before meeting her eyes. "No, Jules. I'd never have done what I did if I hadn't caught him with another girl. You deserved so much better than that asshole. Still do."

"So, that's really why you—"

"Yeah." Sebastian interrupts, advancing further into the room. "He fucking lost it and I knew…I fucking knew right then."

Her gaze snaps between us. "Knew what?"

Fuck. Time to lay it all out here. "He knew I had feelings for you. That's why I went crazy. I didn't want you to find out he was cheating on you, so I forced him to end things. It was better for you to think I was a dick than get your heart broken."

"And why would Sebastian make you promise not to be with me?" she whispers, wrapping her arms around herself.

I glance at Sebastian before my eyes settle on Jules. Her eyes are still wide with shock, but she's also examining me with open curiosity. "Because he knew I was no good for you. That I'd only break your heart. It's why I've been such an asshole all these years. It was easier to resist you if you hated me, and that kept me safe. Kept you safe. I'm so sorry, Jules, about everything."

"Your apology means nothing. I'm sure you said it countless times over the years before slipping out of all those other beds." Bash takes a step toward me, forcing me to back up. "You'll stick your dick in anything with tits. My sister is different. She's not some fucking plaything you get to fuck around with."

"You're right." I hold his gaze, my voice rising. "She is more. More than just another notch on my bedpost, more than just a fuck. Why do you think I could never commit to anyone? Why do you think, Bash? No one could fucking compare. I'd have given Jules the world.

Chapter 11

She's everything. She always has been. She didn't deserve some asshole who couldn't keep it in his pants. She deserves someone who knows how damn special she is and would treat her right. I would have done that. Fuck, Bash, even though I didn't deserve her, I'd have never used her."

Bash and Julia fall into silence, evidently lost in the aftermath of the bomb I just dropped. I can't find it in me to give a shit. It's taken ten years, but I pulled my head out of my ass and put my heart on the line. I did the right thing and will accept whatever fate has in store for me. There's a good chance I just lost them both. But I don't want to live with any more secrets. I don't have it in me to pretend anymore.

Sebastian takes another step toward me and shakes his head. "I'm trying really hard not to punch you in the face right now. You need to get your shit and get the fuck out of here."

I glance toward Jules, who's frozen in place, and nod. "Yeah. I'll go."

Keeping the pillow tight against my crotch, I edge past Bash. From the doorway, I peer at Julia one last time. Her bright amber eyes glisten with unshed tears. She may not want to hear anymore, but I have to say it, at least once.

"Jules, I love you. Anyways have."

And then I'm gone. I'm only half paying attention as I pull on some jeans and a sweater and throw the rest of my stuff in my suitcase. I manage to remember to call a cab. It's too cold to walk to my parent's house, and I don't need frostbite on top of everything else.

I didn't do flowers, romance, commitment or any of that other lovey-dovey bullshit, but maybe I want to. Maybe I'm ready to change. Jules has always made me want more. Want to be more.

Thanks to her brother and my own cowardice I'll never have the chance.

The cab honks from outside, and I make my way downstairs. I pause in front of the Christmas tree, take a package out of the front of my suitcase, and slip a present for Julia under her tree.

"Merry Christmas, Sweets."

12

JULES

❄

I should get up, get dressed, get moving, but I'm still frozen in place on my bed, clutching the comforter to my naked breasts. Sebastian tucked tail and ran off as soon as Nash left. Nash. Fuck. I'm not ready for complicated. I never asked for this. It was supposed to be one night of fun before we both cut strings and pretended nothing ever happened.

Now what? How can I pretend our night together was meaningless?

He loves me? He's always loved me?

My heart pounds in my chest as it dawns on me. It makes sense. What he did to Colby, how he's acted all these years, all the women. I just—I don't know how to process. I didn't even think he liked me, let alone loved me.

I crawl out of bed and throw on a pair of red and black plaid leggings and a white slouchy sweater, and make my way downstairs. Sebastian's on the couch, hunched forward with his head resting in his hands.

"I feel like I should say I'm sorry." I stop in front of him, wringing my hands in front of me. "I didn't mean to destroy your friendship with Nash."

Sebastian raises his head, his eyes full of anguish. "You don't have to apologize. You're a grown woman and can do whoever you want."

I wince before sitting down next to him. "Neither one of us planned on anything happening. And we definitely didn't want you to find out."

"Well, that makes me feel a whole lot better."

"Sorry," I mumble as I reach out to rub his shoulder.

He hangs his head, giving it a slight shake, before meeting my eyes. "I think I should be the one apologizing to you."

"What?"

Sebastian pulls a perfectly wrapped present, complete with bow, from the other side of him and places it in my lap.

With a furrowed brow, I look from the gift and then back to him. "What's this?"

"I don't know." He sighs and leans back, crossing his feet at the ankles. "I found it when I came downstairs. It's from Nash."

"Nash? I'm surprised you didn't throw it in the trash." Or drive over to his parent's house to throw it back in his face.

Sebastian chuckles to himself. "I thought about it. You should open it."

I drop my gaze to the silver and gold package sitting in my lap. I turn it over in my hands, wondering what in the hell kind of gift Nash would leave for me. Before I can let nerves get the better of me, I rip it open.

Curious. It's some sort of book. I open it and start turning pages before my fingers still and all I can do is stare down in amazement. No, he didn't. This is incredible. He made a book of the countless Christmas photos I'd taken over the years. Including one of him and Sebastian dressed as angels. He hunted down every copy of that picture and destroyed them, or at least, that's what I thought.

Tears fall down, blurring into the paper surrounding the pictures, and I reach up to swipe at them. This is the best, most thoughtful, gift anyone has ever given me.

"See." Sebastian nudges me with his elbow before running his hands through his hair. "I think I owe the both of you an apology. I was too blind to see that he cares about you. I always thought he had this infatuation with you that didn't go beyond sex. I was wrong. I won't stand in your way. If you want Nash, go get him. Bring him home for Christmas. I need someone to keep me company while I supervise you making dinner."

I hold the album to my chest, over the heart threatening to beat out of my chest. "I don't know what to think. I don't know what I want."

"Are you sure about that?"

As I clutch the sweetest Christmas present ever, given to me by the one man who drives me crazier than anyone else on the planet, I realize I know what I want.

Last night changed things for me, changed how I see Nash. Being with him felt right. Safe. It felt like home. I haven't felt like that since before my parent's accident.

Can it really be that simple? Can Nash be the link to my happiness?

13

JULES

❄

I WIPE my hands down the front of my leggings. I'm so nervous my damn palms are sweating, and I can barely hear anything above the pounding of my heart. Who knew creating your own Christmas miracle would be so nerve-racking?

Before I can raise my hand to knock on the door, it pulls open. Nash stands at the doorway, his hand gripping the door, and his eyes searching my face. Being close to him has my body buzzing with excitement.

"Jules." He walks out on the porch, closing the door behind him. "What are you doing here?"

"Am I interrupting?" I point to the door. "Were you going somewhere?"

He shakes his head before pinning me in place with his ocean blue stare. "No. I mean, yes. I was on my way to see you. I didn't like how I left. I thought we should talk. I'm surprised to see you here. Does Bash know?"

I take a step closer to him and lay a hand on his forearm. "It's okay. Sebastian knows. He actually suggested it. I think your super sweet present won him over."

Nash closes his eyes and relaxes his shoulders before his lids steadily raise. "What about you?"

"I don't know, Nash. We agreed to one night."

"I know."

"You never do more than one night."

"I know." The anguish in his voice rests heavy in my heart. "But I want to, with you."

Nash reaches out, framing the sides of my face with his hands, and peers into my eyes as if he were silently begging me to admit the same thing. I feel like I'm the last one at the party. I don't know what took me so long to see this different side to Nash. To realize we always gravitated toward each other. To see how he would do anything for me, including changing his lifestyle.

"I want more than one night, too."

He strokes a hand along my jaw, running his thumb over my bottom lip. "What did you say?"

I take a deep breath. If he can lay everything on the line, so can I. It didn't take long after I opened his gift for me to come to my senses. The reason Nash affects me so much is because I love him, too. Always have. I held on to all the hatred, shrouded myself in it so I didn't have to face the truth.

But he's not the man I thought he was, he's better.

"Since you're obviously hard of hearing, I said I want more than one night with you."

He brings his forehead down to mine, framing my

face with his hands, his breath caressing my lips. "I want everything with you."

We stand there staring into each other's eyes with goofy smiles on our faces until Nash breaks the silence. "What should we do now?"

"Well." I point up to the mistletoe pinned above our heads. "I think it's tradition if two people are under the mistletoe, they kiss. I could be wrong, but I don't feel like I am."

"Is it now?" A smile stretches across his face as he slides his hand down my back and pulls me against him. "I can't argue with tradition."

His mouth smashes down to mine, and I wrap my arms around his neck. This feels right. He feels right. I open up to him and his tongue sweeps in my mouth, gliding along the length of mine. His kiss is greedy, like he can't get enough, and I meet him stroke for stroke. His tongue is warm and tastes like hot chocolate. And I know, I just know, I'll never be able to get enough of him.

Nash pulls back, placing kisses along my jaw. "Come on. Let's go back home. We've got a holiday to celebrate, and as much as I want you to myself, we can't leave Bash alone."

I nod before raising up and giving him a quick peck. "And maybe later I'll let you unwrap your Christmas present."

"Oh, yeah? What is it?"

I raise my brows and pull him to the car. "Me."

"That's perfect, because all I want for Christmas is you, Sweets," he sings the last bit doing his best—

maybe his worst—Mariah Carey impression. He slips his arms around my waist, presses my back to his chest and kisses my cheek with several loud kisses. "I love you."

"I love you, too." I wiggle my ass against his denim covered cock and throw him a look over my shoulder. "Now get your ass in the car. You can unwrap me later. I'm also going to hide mistletoe all over the house. I think it would give us a treat all year round."

The smirk says it all. Looks like Christmas miracles do come true. And my Christmas miracle has a low, terrible singing voice that follows me all the way to the car as he belts out *All I Want For Christmas Is You*.

EPILOGUE
NASH

One Year Later

❄

"How are we doing over there, cupcake?" Sebastian grins at me, and I want to punch him. Right in his smug little face.

He knows exactly how I'm doing. I'm fucking nervous as hell, and if I were the kind of guy to have panic attacks, I'd be breathing into a paper bag at an alarming rate. I can't believe guys willingly do this. He's been here all day helping me turn Jules' living room—well, our living room after I moved in last month—into her own winter wonderland.

We've got trees set up on either side of the fireplace, twinkle lights and poinsettias everywhere, and more mistletoe than I've ever seen hanging from every square inch of the ceiling. I think it's romantic, but then again,

I'm not my audience. Jules has to love it. She will love it.

"You should see yourself right now." He points at me and laughs, which is super helpful. "You've got these crazy eyes and I think you're twitching. Are you twitching?"

"I'm trying not to punch you," I ground out.

Sebastian throws his head back and his shoulders shake with laughter. "No, I don't think that's it. I don't think I've ever seen you like this. In fact, I should take a picture." He digs out his phone and shakes it in front of my face, tempting me to charge him. "The great Nashton Wyatt without all his unshakable confidence."

"I have plenty of confidence." I cast him a sideways glance before I round the Christmas trees, adjusting and fluffing the branches as I go. "You're an asshole. I hope you know that."

He holds up his phone and snaps a few pictures of the room, including me, his face reflecting pure delight. "I know, and I'm enjoying every minute of it. This is great for me."

"Shouldn't you be leaving?"

He glances at his phone and frowns. "Yeah, you're right. Damn. I should get going. I was hoping to have more time to harass you. I'll just have to do it tomorrow. Maybe get us some beer you can cry into when my sister rejects you."

"Get the fuck out of here." Ignoring him, I go back to manipulating the tree branches until the door closes behind him.

I hang my head and blow out a long sigh as I move

across the room and throw myself down on the couch. She could definitely reject me, that's a real possibility. And it scares the shit out of me. I've never been close to a moment like this. Never lived with a girl before either. There's a first time for everything and Jules took a lot of my firsts. Not the sexual ones—although there were a few of those—but the important ones. And if tonight works out, she'll be my last too.

She should be home any minute now.

I push up from the couch and cross the room, turning out the lights so everything is illuminated by the iridescent glow of the pale, white twinkling lights. The small velvet box sits heavy in my pocket, and I trace its outline through the black slacks.

The doorknob jostles as it turns, and I move to stand between the two sparkling trees. Coming into the entryway, she closes the door behind her, takes off her jacket, tosses it on the back of the couch, and freezes. She looks around the room with widened eyes, taking in the glimmering lights, the poinsettias, and the dangling mistletoe before her gaze settles on me.

"What is all this?" She gestures to the room, her voice tinged with awe. "Are we starting a new Christmas Eve tradition?"

"Not exactly." I shift on my feet and my hand goes back to tracing the ring box.

Jules eyes me curiously and moves toward me. "Then what is it?"

I take a step forward and grab her hands, holding them between us. "Jules, you are the light of my life. You make me do ridiculous things like string lights and hang mistletoe. You make me love you more every single day. You make me be a better man. Your man."

I pull out the small velvet box before bending down to get on one knee. Jules' eyes gleam with unshed tears and she presses a hand over her heart. "Nash."

"Julia Lauren Rowe, I love you more than life itself. Will you do me the honor of becoming my wife?" I open the ring box and Jules gasps.

It took me months to find the perfect ring. It's a princess cut set in a platinum band with antique swirls. The diamond is a bit on the larger side as I don't do anything half-assed, but the expression on her face tells me I picked a good one.

Jules kneels down in front of me, a tear running down her cheek, and I reach out with my thumb to wipe it away. It hasn't escaped my notice I haven't gotten an answer yet but hope she's overwhelmed and not about to rip my heart out.

"Nash." Jules reaches out to stroke a hand down the side of my face. "I love you. Of course, I'll be your wife."

"I know I can be difficult. I know—wait, did you say yes?" Her words finally sink into my man-brain and a smile spreads across my face.

She nods.

With a shaky hand, I pluck the ring from the box and slide it on Jules' ring finger. It looks perfect. And in the glow of the lights, surrounded by mistletoe, and my love, she looks absolutely radiant. I take her face between my hands, and bring my mouth to hers, kissing her softly with light caresses of my lips.

Epilogue

I pull back and gaze into her bright amber eyes. "I'm going to make you so happy, future Mrs. Wyatt."

"You already make me happy."

I bring my mouth back down to hers, sliding my tongue past the seam of her lips, pushing her to the floor and covering her with my body. Her hands stroke my face and I can feel the band of the ring sitting on her finger. She already makes me happy, too. Happier than I ever thought possible. I don't deserve this. I don't deserve her.

But I'll never let her go.

***

Thank you for reading MISTLETOE AND MISCHIEF-I hope you enjoyed Nash and Jules's journey as much as I enjoyed writing it! Do you want to read more from Melissa Ivers? Check out the Nashville Devils hockey team! FORBIDDEN DEVIL features Lincoln and Jazz, a laugh-out-loud, second chance, forbidden romance with plenty of steam, and a dirty talking alpha that has it bad for his tight skirt wearing boss. Keep reading for a special sneak peek.

Want to stay in the know about all my upcoming releases? Just sign up for my newsletter.

As an Indie Author, I would love your help spreading the word about MISTLETOE AND MISCHIEF. If you enjoyed the story please consider leaving a review on Amazon, Goodreads, or even referring to a friend. Even a sentence or two makes a huge difference.

Thank you for taking this journey with me.
Melissa

※

One-Click FORBIDDEN DEVIL

FORBIDDEN DEVIL -PREVIEW

From CHAPTER ONE
Jazz

The ballots were sent out, votes cast, and results tallied. The consensus, ladies and gentlemen—*drum roll, please*—the general manager is a giant dick. Side note—probably overcompensating for a small one.

Resident asshole in question, Adam Barrett, GM of the Nashville Devils hockey team, sits across the conference room table from my brother and I in an awkward stare down. To say I could slash the tension with a machete would be a gross understatement.

Damn, I'd love to have one of those right now. Self-defense is alive and well in Tennessee.

While Adam is a pretty decent GM, he's a shit human being.

"I don't know what you both expect from me." Adam plants his hands on the long mahogany table and leans toward us. His chair creaks beneath him, and he lets out a frustrated sigh. Every word he speaks drips with contempt. "It's not in my job description to babysit two over-privileged rich kids who can't fathom what it means to own a hockey franchise, let alone run it."

Epilogue

I shift in my chair and my pulse skyrockets, as the heated glare from Adam settles on me. His hardened brown eyes bore into my soul, and I swear I can hear his teeth crack beneath the pressure of his clenched jaw.

It's a good thing looks can't actually kill. If they could, my lifeless corpse would slouch to the floor.

I did not wear my kickass heels to die in them.

Adam will have to glare me to death another day.

He'd been my father's right-hand man for years, and for the life of me, I don't understand why. Not that my father and I had a particularly close relationship. Growing up, I was always my mother's problem. Even after they divorced, he was too busy to spend real quality time with his children. But if the rumors are true, he was just as difficult as Adam, and Adam is a dumpster fire. Being an asshole must be a fairly common trait in the upper echelons of men's professional hockey.

I glance at my brother. Gordon's widened eyes and rigid posture reflect the same shock I feel.

Well, this meeting is off to a fantastic start.

Gordon and I set up this appointment with every intention of aligning ourselves with Adam, wanting to get the upper management team on the same page before our ownership was announced to the country. Somewhere in the last five minutes, the train left the station, derailed, and plowed into a fireworks factory.

I eye him like I would a ticking time bomb. I'm sure he won't physically explode, even though the pulsing vein on the side of his forehead indicates otherwise. "We're not trying to cause you more work."

"It doesn't matter. You're going to," Adam growls.

I hold my hands up in surrender. "Listen, Adam—"

"What would a spoiled princess like you know about hockey, anyway? You probably wouldn't know a puck if it hit you in the face." He gestures toward me, his hand sweeping out before it falls back to the table with a loud thump.

Considering I grew up playing hockey, I can only assume his observation is based purely on the fact I have a vagina and not my actual experience with the sport. I'm also pretty sure he knows that.

He's a fucking prick.

"I did play hockey. In the Olympics."

"On the *women's* team. We all know how different it is from real hockey."

I steal a glance at Gordon. His green eyes sharpen, his nostrils flare, and his lips press together in a firm line. He's always the first one to come to my defense. Not that I can't stand up for myself, but in his mind, no one messes with his little sister. Adam is either completely oblivious, or doesn't give a shit, because he turns to him next.

"And you, Gordie." He spits out the name like my brother doesn't deserve to share a name with the great hockey legend. "You're just some washed up has-been who couldn't make it in pro-hockey. You're sure as shit not going to hack it here."

My spine straightens, and I throw my shoulders back as the blood simmers in my veins. If there's anyone who needs to eat a bag of dicks, it's this guy.

Gordon is a lot of things, but a washed-up has-been

isn't one of them. The only reason he isn't playing professional hockey is a devastating knee injury. Otherwise, he'd still be out there week after week tearing up the ice.

He stands, towering over Adam with his bulky six-foot-three frame. The muscle in his jaw tics before he leans over and slaps his hands flat on the table. The sound echoes off the walls as he pins Adam with a glare, and I give him a mental high five. It's a total power move to put Adam back in his place.

He needs to learn he's no longer in charge around here.

"Unfortunately for you, *Mr. Barrett*, our father left the hockey team to us. In case you don't understand, that means you now answer to Jazlyn and me. It would be in your best interest to keep future comments about our perceived shortcomings to yourself." Gordon straightens, smoothing a hand down his tie. "Unless, of course, you'd like to search for another NHL team to work for. I don't know anyone who's looking for a new GM right now, and with last season's record, you don't look too good."

Adam's face turns a satisfying shade of red as he jumps to his feet. "What the hell was your father thinking? You two are going to be the end of this team. You're both a laughingstock. Don't think we aren't all waiting for you to fail." With one last glare at Gordon, then me, Adam turns and stalks out of the room, slamming the door behind him.

My fists clench under the table so hard my nails dig into my palms. I want nothing more than to charge into his office and tear him a new asshole. But regardless of how I feel about Adam, we need him. My father's closed mind and selfishness brought the Devils to the bottom. They finished the previous season with the second worst record in the league. Pair those stats with two inexperienced owners, no general manager in their right mind would consider joining the organization right now. We need to win, and win often, to entice even a half-decent GM to replace Adam.

That means my best option is to swallow my pride and let it go. Even if my brain is screaming at me to clean house.

Gordon releases a long breath, unbuttons his black suit jacket, and collapses into his seat. Dark circles rim his eyes, and there's a noticeable slouch in his shoulders. He looks like he's in need of a serious nap, or maybe a stiff drink. Or both.

I need both.

"That went well," I muse, lacing my fingers together in front of me, and quirk my mouth in a wry smile.

"I don't know, sis. I'm not sure we were in the same meeting."

I hate how Adam makes him sound so defeated, and it riles me up all over again. I shoot to my feet, sending my chair rolling several feet backward. "You know what? Fuck that guy. I don't give a shit what he says. We're going to turn this team around. This is *our* legacy, Gordon. We're going to take the Devils out of the bottom and make them winners. We're going to prove everyone wrong, including that fancy suit wearing asshole." My voice steels with resolve as I point towards the door where Adam made his recent exit.

Gordon slumps even lower and runs a hand down his face. "I hope you're right, Jazz. I really hope you're right."

"I think you should know by now, brother, I'm always right." My lips curl up in a smirk, and I cock my hip against the table.

Am I cocky? Yes. A little self-assured? Right now, absolutely.

But the gauntlet has been thrown, and there's no way in hell I'm not picking it up. Just need to figure out how to run a hockey franchise while simultaneously building a good team and getting wins.

Couldn't be too hard. Probably. Right?

Gordon shakes his head, chuckling. "I wish we could just fire him."

"Trust me, I know the feeling. Unfortunately, unless we can start winning, I don't think we stand a chance at recruiting anyone."

"True enough." Gordon makes his way to the door of the conference room. "I'm going to make some calls to a few friends of mine and see what our options are for replacing him."

I nod. "Good idea. Keep me posted."

Anger and restlessness boil through me. Sitting down in my office chair to stew for the next few hours doesn't seem very productive. A good walk around the stadium will help me get my bearings and settle the storm brewing inside.

Adam's right about one thing. I have no idea what it

takes to run a hockey team. For the better part of my twenty-eight years of life, I've been on the ice. The front of the house is foreign to me, and I didn't ask for it. I didn't expect to have a hockey team suddenly thrown in my lap. I didn't expect to have to move my entire life for Dad's dying wish, or for his dying wish to land me as co-owner of his hockey team.

I certainly didn't expect to be in a position where I would be completely disregarded and disrespected because of my gender. Our ownership hasn't even been made public yet. If Adam's reaction is any indication, I'm in for a media shit show.

Great.

I make it downstairs, sure I'll be able to find the workout room and, with it, a punching bag. Maybe giving it hell for a few minutes will improve my mood. Better it than Adam's face. I clench and unclench my fists. I haven't been this pissed in a long time.

Lost in my violent thoughts, I round a corner and run into a solid wall of muscle. The impact sends me staggering in my heels, and I might have fallen on my ass if two hands didn't reach out to steady me.

"I'm so sorry."

My muscles tense, and my heart pounds in my chest. I know that voice. It's deep and gritty, yet smooth and hypnotizing. It's a voice I could get lost in. And have. The meeting with Adam threw me off balance, and I forgot about him being here.

As one of my players.

"I almost ran you over. Are you okay?" A flicker of

recognition sparks in his light blue eyes, and his hands drop to his sides.

Lincoln Dallas.

A missed opportunity if there ever was one. One look at him, one innocent touch, has my nipples peaked and my panties soaked. My body remembers him too.

He's one of the sexiest men I've ever laid eyes on. His tall, muscled body, full lips, and chiseled jaw are a gift to women everywhere. The hockey gods have been kind to him. Unlike some of the other hockey players, he doesn't look like he just got knocked around a few times after meeting the wrong end of a hockey stick.

"Jazz?" Lincoln's mouth tilts to a frown. "What are you doing here?"

One-Click FORBIDDEN DEVIL

ALSO BY MELISSA IVERS

Devils Hockey
FORBIDDEN DEVIL (Lincoln and Jazz)
RECKLESS DEVIL (Tag and Elle)

Love in Aspen
MISTLETOE AND MISCHIEF (Nash and Jules)

ACKNOWLEDGMENTS

I am so grateful to have great people willing to be with me from start to finish. I've pulled people to just sit with me and talk things out, read through something I'm not sure of, critique me when I think something's garbage, and help make it better.

So, all you bitches that helped me, I want to say thank you, from the bottom of my heart. You know who you are, but in case you need me to say it, because you're a drama llama... A huge thank you to Beth and Krista, (My Catique Kitties), Brittany, the most awesome PA there is, the Lady D's Danielle, Marissa and Rachel, and my family for putting up with all my deadlines and hours I dedicate to writing.

A HUGE thank you to all the reviewers and bloggers for reading the story and helping me spread the word about my story.

And I especially want to thank you! Thank you for reading. Thank you for making it to the end. And hopefully, thank you for loving it.

Melissa

ABOUT THE AUTHOR

Lover of all things romance and hockey, she also loves to bake extra delicious treats. Melissa Ivers loves to write steamy stories with all those hot, alpha men and women who can bring them to their knees literally and figuratively. Melissa lives in Kentucky with her eye-rolling teenage son and two of the laziest dogs known to man. She has numerous fictional boyfriends, but—shhhh—they don't know about each other.

When she isn't writing or working, you'll find her under a blanket on the couch reading a book off Kindle. She also likes baking yummy treats for family and friends, binge watching shows off Netflix, such as the *Office* and *Vampire Diaries* and being an all-around joy.

To keep current with what Melissa is doing stalk her on social media or check out her websites

Facebook
Instagram
Website

Looking to stay in touch and keep up with my new

releases, sales and promotions? Join my Newsletter and my facebook reader group Melissa's Sweet and Sassy Readers. I'd love to see you there.

Printed in Great Britain
by Amazon